Harry Dickson

THE AMERICAN SHERLOCK HOLMES
The Man in Grey

IN THE SAME SERIES

Harry Dickson – *The Heir of Dracula*
Harry Dickson – *vs. The Spider*
Harry Dickson – *The Werewolf of Rutherford Grange*
Sherlock Holmes vs. Fantômas (play)

BY ARNOULD GALOPIN

Doctor Omega
The Man with the Blue Face

THE AMERICAN SHERLOCK HOLMES
The Man in Grey

by
Arnould Galopin

From The Secret Files of The King of Detectives
adapted and retold in English by
Jean-Marc & Randy Lofficier

A Black Coat Press Book

Acknowledgements: We are indebted to Stephan Martiniere and Marc Madouraud.

Visit our website at www.blackcoatpress.com

TABLE OF CONTENTS

LES ROMANS MYSTÉRIEUX
ARNOULD GALOPIN
L'homme au Complet gris
Éditions Jules TALLANDIER
75, Rue Dareau, Paris-14e

Introduction

L'Homme au Complet Gris, translated here as *The Man in Grey,* was first serialized in *Le Journal* from 23 May to 25 June 1911, and was subsequently published in book form by Tallandier in 1912.

It starred the character of Allan Dickson, nick-named "The King of Australian Detectives," a hero created by Arnould Galopin under the pseudonym of "Max Dearly."[1]

Allan Dickson made his first appearance in four short stories, all published in the magazine *Mon Beau Livre* by Arthème Fayard:

* No.10 (Oct. 1906): *L'Alibi*

* No.11 (Nov. 1906): *La Main du Diable* [The Devil's Hand]

* No.13 (Jan. 1907): *L'Hôtel de Broadway* [The Broadway Hotel]

* No.16 (Apr. 1907): *L'Affaire de Grosvenor House* [The Grosvenor House Affair][2]

The character proved successful enough for Galopin to bring him back in a full-blown novel, *La Ténébreuse Affaire de Green Park* [The Murky Affair of Green Park], serialized in *Le Journal* in June 1910, then reprinted in book form by Tallandier in 1911.

---

[1] For more information regarding Arnould Galopin, please refer to our edition of *Doctor Omega*, Black Coat Press, ISBN 978-1-0-9740711-1-4.

[2] A fifth story entitled *L'Assurance sur la Vie* [Life insurance] was announced but not published.

The following year, roughly concurrently with the serial publication of *L'Homme au Complet Gris*, Galopin wrote another serial featuring Allan Dickson, entitled *Ténébras, Le Bandit Fantôme* [Tenebras, The Phantom Bandit],[3] an imitation of the then-hugely popular *Fantômas*. *Ténébras* first appeared as 42 fascicules published by La Librairie Contemporaine, then was collected in book form by Tallandier in 1912.

After that, Allan Dickson made another appearance in *La Sandale Rouge* [The Red Sandal], also serialized in *Le Journal* in 1913 (24 Oct.-6 Dec.), before making room for more serious works about the Great War, including the classic *Sur le Front de Mer* [*On the Sea Front*] (1918), a critically-acclaimed novel about the Merchant Navy, which won Galopin the Grand Prize of the French Academy.

But Galopin never entirely let go of Allan Dickson, who returned, sometimes in mere cameo roles, in several of his subsequent works:

* *Les Suites d'un Mariage d'Amour* [The Sequels of a Love Marriage], serialized in Le Journal 24 Oct.-19 Dec. 1924, reprinted in book form by Albin Michel in 1929;

* the serial *Le Petit Detective*, 69 fascicules out of 83 in total written by Galopin, and published by Albin Michel between 1934-37, in which Dickson met Jean Tixier, the eponymous hero, as well as another of Galopin's characters, the "Lupinian" Edgar Pipe;

* *Le Mystère de Clarence Terrace*, which was published posthumously in *Le Journal* from 21 July to 21 August 1936. (Galopin had passed away on 8 December 1934.)

---

[3] To be published next by Black Coat Press.

Allan and Harry

Could Allan Dickson and Harry Dickson be one and the same?

Yes.

The literary origins of Harry Dickson are detailed in Black Coat Press' first collection devoted to his adventures, *The Heir of Dracula*, which also includes a profile of the character and a timeline. Suffice it to say here that the series of pulp magazines which eventually became *Harry Dickson* began in Germany in January 1907 under the title of *Detektiv Sherlock Holmes und Seine Weltberühmten Abenteuer* (*Sherlock Holmes and His Most Famous Cases*).

The fact that the name of Sherlock Holmes was used on the cover created some concern about the wrath of Sir Arthur Conan Doyle's lawyers, and, with No. 11, the series was retitled *Aus den Geheimakten des Weltdetektivs* (*The Secret Files of the King of Detectives*), even though, inside, the main characters were still called Sherlock Holmes and Doctor Watson. The stodgy Watson, however, was soon replaced by a younger and more dynamic character named Harry Taxon.

The series ran for 230 weekly issues, ending in March 1911, with covers by the renowned Berlin Academy artist Alfred Roloff.

Sixteen issues of the German series were then adapted into French in 1907-08, but it was only when the Dutch-Flemish publisher Roman-Boek-en-Kunsthandel relaunched the series in December 1927 with Dutch translations of the original German, that the names of "Harry Dickson" and "Tom Wills" (his young assistant) appeared for the first time.

The following year, Belgian publisher Hippolyte Janssens decided to translate the Dutch series into French, entrusting the job to renowned Belgian author Jean Ray, starting with its 20th issue. The French series began in January 1929 and lasted 178 issues, until April 1938. The Roloff covers, which had been purchased in bulk from the German publisher, greatly contributed to its success.

Some scholars have speculated that the name "Harry Dickson" was a logical derivation from that of "Harry Taxon." But others have remarked upon the similarities between Harry Dickson and the already-popular Allan Dickson, one being advertised the "American Sherlock Holmes," the other as the "Australian Sherlock Holmes." After all, it was not as if the publishers of Harry Dickson had not already proven that they were more than willing to "borrow" shamelessly from previous sources!

As far as Black Coat Press is concerned, at some point, it became too tempting for the writers of our series *Tales of the Shadowmen* to assume that the two Dicksons were indeed one and the same.

G.L. Gick provided an explanation for the similarities in his story *The Werewolf of Rutherford Grange*,[4] which takes place in the summer of 1911, when Dickson is apprenticing with another legendary detective, Sexton Blake, and teams up with the mystic Sâr Dubnotal:

"As a matter of fact, I am related to Allan," [said Dickson.] *"Quite closely. He's me. That is, Allan's my middle name. I went by it for a time a few years ago."*

"I see," replied Miss Gianetti, *"but you're American."*

---

[4] Black Coat Press, ISBN 978-1-935558-80-4.

"Oh, that's very easy to explain. My father was a magician. While touring in Sydney, he met my mother. In my youngest years, I spoke much like her..."

According to Galopin in *La Ténébreuse Affaire de Green Park*, Allan Dickson's father was named Edgar Arthur Dickson and was a well-known farmer in Western Australia, before being murdered, thus launching young Allan, like Bruce Wayne, on his crime-fighting career. Harry Dickson's family background, on the other hand, remains unknown. We know, however, that Arsène Lupin studied magic with a stage magician named Dickson in Paris in 1893.[5]

Perhaps Harry Dickson's father was Dickson the magician? This would explain Harry's skills of legerdemain, as well as the fact that he was educated mostly in boarding schools. And Dickson the magician might have met his wife while on tour in Sidney, bought some farmland, and eventually met his sad fate there, thus creating another champion of justice.

Dickson and Holmes

In 1906, at age 18, Harry Dickson fought the archvillain Fantômas who had just tried to kill Sherlock Holmes. That story is told in the 1914 stage play *Sherlock Holmes vs. Fantômas* by Pierre de Wattyne &

---

[5] Information provided during the trial of Arsène Lupin in the short story *L'Evasion d'Arsène Lupin* in *Arsène Lupin, Gentleman Cambrioleur*. The real-life Dickson (1857-1939) was a stage magician and some of his props are preserved today at the museum of the Maison de la Magie in Blois.

Yorril Walter.[6] This was Harry Dickson's first encounter with both Holmes and Fantômas.

The affair of *The Man in Grey* recorded by Galopin takes place four years later, in 1910, pretty much at the same time as its publication. In it, Dickson meets a 54-year-old Sherlock Holmes, rechristened "Herlokolms" in the original text by Galopin.

Holmes, who had already been much impressed by the young detective's earlier exploits, if one takes into account the Wattyne & Walter play—but such an untold previous encounter is also mentioned in Galopin's novel—agrees to mentor him before (according to Gick) passing him to Sexton Blake.

The Man in Grey, therefore, fits well in the chronologies of both characters. We have provided a more detailed timeline at the end of this volume, which also includes relevant information about other fictional characters who are also featured in our version of the novel. And we look forward to seeing you again in our next volume in which the fearless young Dickson will clash with the deadly Tenebras...

Jean-Marc & Randy Lofficier

---

[6] Black Coat Press, ISBN 978-1-934543-67-2.

THE MAN IN GREY

CHAPTER I
The Lyndhurst Murder

From the Journals of Harry Dickson
Monday, June 6, 1910.

"It's exactly 1:23 p.m., Mr. Dickson."

"Thank you, Captain."

And we simultaneously repocketed our time pieces.

The *Columbia* was entering Southampton harbor.

I had just lost a ten pound bet with the Captain, but truthfully, I was not sorry, since the accurate time of our arrival—the object of our bet—would enable me to catch the express from the South Western Railway which would have me in London at 3:57 p.m.

The gangplank was lowered and the ship came to a groaning standstill with a last hiss of steam.

On the docks was the milling throng that always accompanied the arrival of any transatlantic steamer. I looked at its diversity with the satisfaction of a man whom, by trade, must learn to recognize and memorize every minute detail around him.

As a matter of fact, I was thrilled to be back in England after three sweaty months spent in New York, the unpleasant city of my birth, with my cousin Frederick.

I said my good-byes to the Captain, whose company I had genuinely enjoyed, and stepped briskly onto the gangplank.

Before me, a clergyman was cautiously making his way with carefully measured steps, grasping the guardrail with a shaky hand. In front of him was an imposing woman, dressed in the bright colors favored by some of the less tasteful citizens of my native America; she carried a small handbag decorated with bizarre flowers intertwined with monograms.

I was forced to follow the measured steps taken by the clergyman in the wake of the imposing lady.

On the docks, the porters began hassling us, but far from being bothered, I was thrilled to recognize in their strong accents the sounds of an England which I had always cherished.

While we made our way towards customs, slowly, in a beeline, someone came up from behind me and tried to elbow his way through. I heard the muttered protests of the other passengers who, like me, had been politely staying in line behind the imposing woman.

The man rushed past me, swearing under his breath against everything and everyone, making irritated gestures; he was dressed in the type of old-fashioned waterproof coat that the English only wear in vaudeville shows.

Once on the ground, he began hailing the porters, calling loudly—but unsuccessfully. By his accent and poor pronunciation, I knew him at once to be French.

I approached the man and, thanks to the time I had spent on holidays in *la belle France* with Antoine de Hautefeuille, I was able to address him in reasonably fluent French.

"Monsieur is visibly in a hurry," I said, while hailing a man, "and needs a porter to help him with his luggage."

The Frenchman expressed his gratitude profusely, even grabbing my arm in their typically familiar manner, but I disengaged myself and, after tipping my hat, I left him with the rest of the crowd.

After going through customs, as I made my progress towards the railway station, I heard the shouts of the paper boys hawking the noon edition of the newspapers, which featured in big bold letters the words: *The Lyndhurst Horror*, promising all kinds of gory revelations inside.

That was enough for me to become a detective again. I bought a paper and quickly began reading it.

It was indeed a murder, and an exceptionally challenging case by the look of it.

"Good," I thought. "*He* must certainly be there already."

I changed my mind; I wouldn't be going to London after all. I shouted to the porter who had been carrying my trunks:

"Take these to the left luggage, please."

In the train, I carefully reread the newspaper article. A woman's body, horribly mutilated, had been found that very morning on the commons in the nearby town of Lyndhurst, about nine miles southwest of Southampton. The police had been summoned and were already busy questioning potential witnesses.

This is a unique opportunity to distinguish myself, I thought. *I couldn't have imagined a better case.* He *will have a chance to see me at work, and won't regret his invitation.*

A couple of hours later, I arrived in Lyndhurst and set out towards the scene of the crime on foot. Many other curious onlookers had stepped off the train with the same purpose in mind, and I had but to follow them.

Lyndhurst is, as is well known, a town favored by golfers and tennis players. The discovery of that awful murder had shocked, even frightened, the local community. Then, morbid curiosity had taken over and compelled the locals to come out in droves to take a peek at the grisly scene.

Englishmen are not by nature prone to being overly emotional, at least not in public. I felt that this display of macabre curiosity was driven less by ghoulish appetite than by the need to ascertain the situation for themselves and, hopefully, see justice done and order reestablished.

The circumstances behind the murder were still a complete mystery, and the good citizens of Lyndhurst sought an explanation, which is why they were converging *en masse* towards the commons.

I walked alongside them and, soon enough, I arrived at a vast grassy rectangle that looked exceptionally well tended and that was bordered by a thicket of woods on one side.

The crowd had gathered in a neat circle around the commons, and was kept at distance from the crime scene by a few local Bobbies. At the center of that circle was a body, or rather something that had once been a body. Kneeling besides it was a man, alone, looking pensive.

I was right. He *is here already*, I thought

I stepped forward with assurance.

"No stepping through," said a huge policeman, extending two arms as wide as beams to bar my way.

I showed him the card upon which *He* had scribbled a few words, extending his invitation.

"Ah, I see... That's another thing then, if you're *his* guest," said the policeman, looking impressed.

He pushed aside a few gawkers, who had seized the opportunity to move forward, in order to let me through.

I walked briskly towards the center of the circle and was, at last, able to get a good view of the body, and of the man who had been studying it—my mentor and spiritual master.

"Mr. Sherlock Holmes!" I said.

"Ah! Mr. Harry Dickson!"

We shook hands vigorously, as two long-lost friends, even though we had only met once before, four years ago.

"I'd guessed that I'd find you here, sir. That's why I came straight from Southampton to Lyndhurst, instead of going to Baker Street."

"An excellent deduction, my dear Harry... I recognize in that the flair of the man who recently solved the murky affair of Green Park."

I bowed, flattered by his acknowledgement of my first big case.

Holmes nodded and put the briar pipe that he had stopped smoking in order to chat with me back in his pocket.

He was a man in his late fifties or early sixties; yet no one would have called him an old man, despite the silvery grey hair that shone beneath his cap. His eyes were so sharp and penetrating that something of their remarkable acuity seemed to linger on a person for a few seconds, even after he had stopped looking at them. He wore no facial hair and his cheeks had been hardened by the use of a steel razor. His jaws occasionally tightened in an involuntary reflex, as if he were grinding his teeth.

I noticed his nervous hands, with heavy veins bulging under his tightly-drawn skin. He was tall and thin, but that, by no means, conveyed the idea of physical weakness; on the contrary, there was a surprising amount of strength in his lanky frame.

I remained silent out of deference to his thoughts.

"What do you think, Harry?" he suddenly asked me, pointing at the corpse.

"It could be a crime of passion."

"That is possible indeed, but look further."

"It's the handiwork of a brute."

"Yes—a man endowed with tremendous strength."

"Almost superhuman, in fact."

We kneeled to take a closer look at the unfortunate thing that had once been a woman. The bone white of her skull showed under her unrecognizable, ravaged face, having resisted the vice-like squeeze that had crushed the rest of her body.

"The victim was a blonde," said Holmes. "Look at the roots."

The ripped hair, like a blood-soaked rag, had been left discarded amongst the viscera and the stomach, taken from a belly gutted open, just below the thorax.

"Yes."

"Judging by her neck and shoulders, she was young."

"I agree."

"And also of modest condition."

My frown signaled my puzzlement, so, with a movement of the chin, Holmes pointed at the little grey boots the victim wore. I bent forward to take a closer look.

"You're right, Mr. Holmes! It's the kind of cheap article that cost less than five shillings. The manufacture is poor. No society lady would wear such shoes. And the heels are well worn too..."

"So, she was a working class woman... Perhaps a servant..."

Prompted by a thought, I looked at the victim's dislocated hand and did not see a wedding band. The direction of my eyes had not escaped the Great Detective, who had at once deduced my purpose.

"Maybe it fell off?" he said. "We must look for it."

"Or she wasn't wearing one. Not every woman wears her wedding band."

"In America, perhaps, my dear Harry, but not here, in the heart of the British countryside." Holmes smiled. "You are no longer in New York, you know. You forgot the patriarchal traditions of our British society."

We each took a closer look at the deceased woman's hands. The right was mostly intact, even though the skin of three fingers had been peeled off. The left hand, however, had been partially torn off, crushed, and—

"The ring finger is missing," said Holmes, already looking for it in the blood-soaked grass.

But, suddenly, the energy seemed to leak out of him, and he became pale and tired-looking. He wiped his forehead with his hand.

"Mr. Holmes! Is there anything wrong, sir?" I inquired.

"Nothing serious... A dizzy spell, nothing more... I overdid it a little today. It pains me to admit it, but I am not as strong as I used to be. My friend, Doctor Watson, warned me that I would pay for my addictions some day... That time has come, I'm afraid, which is why I'm very happy that you answered my invitation."

"I could do nothing less."

"I need more than a collaborator now... I need an heir—a successor perhaps. Someone with whom I can share my methods. You are young, intelligent, your deductive abilities are unmatched... I have followed your cases. You have a great future ahead of you!"

I lowered my eyes before such fulsome praise, and, by so doing, I accidentally caught a glint of something golden.

"I think I've found our missing ring," I said, happy to divert his mind from his morbid thoughts. "Here it is!"

The gold band that had caught my eye was lying a few feet away from the body, partially hidden by the trampled grass. It was still attached to the ring finger.

I presented the gruesome artifact to Holmes.

"That finger was not torn off," he observed. "It was bitten off."

I could not repress a shudder.

"That unfortunate woman may have been fighting off her aggressor," I suggested. "Trying to push him away, her hand may have slipped into his mouth and..."

"...And she lost her finger that way. Yes, it is possible, I suppose," finished Holmes, nodding, but in a listless manner.

"We have already gathered quite a few clues," I continued, trying to engage his interest. "We know that the victim was young, blond, of modest condition, and married. Undoubtedly, she lived or worked nearby, and her husband or her employer will be looking for her, if he isn't already. We should soon learn of her identity."

"My dear Harry," said the Great Detective, "in a case like this, the identity of our victim shall not be of much help to us. This is something we can safely leave to the police. Our task is much more difficult. We must find the murderer."

Then, with some of his old energy back, he continued:

"The victim's friends and relatives can indeed be of tremendous help—if the assassin is among them. But what if he is a complete stranger? Rather than helping us, the same friends and relatives can then turn into impediments, smokescreens that the real murderer can use to better hide from the Law—and the police often don't have enough acumen to see beyond them..."

I sighed and Holmes threw me one of his penetrating glances.

"Of course. You have even better reasons than I to question the police. I read about their mishandling of the Green Park case..."

"Your invitation was not the only incentive I needed to return to England, Mr. Holmes," I said with great sincerity.

Now, Holmes looked pensive. Perhaps his prodigious mind was reviewing the details of my first big case, but somehow I did not think so. His next remark confirmed it.

"Do you know what I'm thinking, Harry?" he asked suddenly.

"I believe that there is something about this case that seems familiar to you. You came to Lyndhurst because you wanted to be sure of something, and now you are. However, what that thing is, I do not know."

"Very good, Harry! You are indeed quite perceptive! The fact that the victim is a poor woman... Young... The horror... The sheer savagery of the crime... Her abominable mutilation beyond human imagination... All this, my dear Harry, reminds me of another dark and sinister case..."

"Which one, sir?"

"Could it be a coincidence? No. I do not believe in such things. It must be *him*," he continued, lost in his thoughts.

Then, he turned his attention towards me again.

"We must look at every fact... Investigate every trail... because, if my theory is correct, this is only the latest in a long series of similar crimes... But before I can be sure, one fact must be ascertained... One fact alone... Is *she* back?"

"She?"

"The *Matilda Briggs*."

"What is the *Matilda Briggs*?"

"What I am going to tell you, Harry, I have shared with no one else before—not even my good friend Watson. This is how much I trust you..."

Now, Holmes was back to being his old self. His penetrating gaze drilled into my eyes and touched me deep in my soul.

Around us, the crowd could not overhear our conversation; yet, a hushed silence seemed to have fallen over the commons, and all conversation had become muted, as if they could sense that a tremendous revelation was about to be made. The onlookers watched us closely, feeling that the answer lie within their reach, trying to divine it from our unreadable faces.

"The *Matilda Briggs* is a ship, Harry," said Holmes. "Not the best of ships, for sure—an old schooner that has sailed every sea, stopped in every harbor, with nothing clean about her. A ship of smugglers, thieves and felons... And every time she moors at a British harbor, blood is spilled. Four years ago, in June 1906, she stopped in London. You were attending the University of South Kensington, at the time, doing odd jobs for Nick Carter. Remember the horrible crime of June 13? A school mistress from Hammersmith, found gutted, crushed, mutilated, just like that poor woman here..."

"Yes, I do remember reading about it at the time!"

"And a year later, the *Matilda Briggs* was in Portsmouth, and the body of another woman was found, ripped, torn apart... The police investigation led nowhere, found no clues..."

My mentor's words struck me as true. There was something here that indeed warranted further inquiry.

"Then, she was in Glasgow in December 1908," Holmes continued, "when a young Irishwoman was found near the harbor, gutted of her bowels, hideously disfigured, her bones crushed as if by giant hands. And last year, in March, the *Matilda Briggs* relaxed in Dover... Just at the same time as the police found two young prostitutes, similarly murdered and dismembered, a day apart from each other... It was quite a scandal in the press. You can't have missed it..."

Indeed, I had not.

"No one connected the murders to that ship?" I asked.

"No," replied Holmes. "In every instance, the investigation was perfunctory because of the social status of the victims, and the cases were closed each time without even a single serious suspect taken into custody."

"I can't say I'm surprised," I replied, still feeling some resentment towards the police.

"However, Scotland Yard secretly put together a description of the murderer. He was obviously a madman, endowed with herculean strength, and, unofficially, some of their inspectors gave him a nickname—one harking back to the most terrible unsolved case in all the history of British law enforcement..."

"You don't mean...?"

"Yes, they nicknamed him—the new Jack the Ripper! But little do they know how right they are..."

I looked at Holmes, dumbfounded.

"What do you mean, *how right they are*? Surely, you can't mean that Jack the Ripper is still at large?"

"I can't say anymore right now, Harry. *This is a story for which the world is not yet prepared*."

So, the elusive monster, the ghostly murderer, was back, just when I had undertaken to assist Sherlock Holmes! He was not a myth, not a legend... Jack the Ripper was a man... He had an identity... And now, we knew he might be a sailor, with a known address: the *Matilda Briggs*, and the monster always sailed in search of new victims, but the police had never found his trail...

A new question arose in my mind.

"But you, sir, why haven't you tried to capture that monster?"

"I did, once," replied Holmes, cracking his long fingers. "I thought the case had been closed. I will tell you the full story at another time... But it is only in the last few years that I became aware of the return of the *Matilda Briggs* to our shores..."

"*Return*?"

"Yes. She was tied to the original murders too. Then, two years ago, I took notice of the murders in Glasgow. That's when I became convinced..."

"Convinced of what?"

But he ignored my question and continued:

"...But, by then, she was already gone and forgotten, like a ghost ship. I kept an eye out for her, watching for her return. My attention was now fully focused on her, but no matter what I did, I could not prevent the murders in Dover... And today, my dear Harry, as I stand before this body, as hideously mutilated as the others, I have almost all the answers to my questions... I only need to find if the *Matilda Briggs* is moored at Southampton."

"But you agree that the author of these crimes is one of her sailors?"

"Of course. It's elementary."

"Then let's call Scotland Yard and arrest them all, and we'll..."

"No, not yet, Harry. I have *almost* all the answers, as I said—not all. I still need proof, and it is you who are going to find that proof for me."

"I?"

"Yes, you. First, you are going to verify that the *Matilda Briggs* is indeed in the port of Southampton. Then, I'll have other tasks for you, but I will give you my instructions later. At this stage, the presence of the *Matilda Briggs* in the waters of Southampton is all the information I need. Now, good bye! Go, go quickly, Harry! Time is of the essence if we are to finally put an end to this dreadful business, once and for all..."

Leaving Holmes to his cogitations, I crossed the commons and left in a hurry, walking as fast as I could towards the station. I did notice, however, that this time, I was no longer treated as an anonymous stranger, but that everyone saluted me with deference.

Such was the benefit of being identified as the Great Detective's latest assistant.

Half an hour later, I was traveling at full steam towards Southampton on the South Western Railway.

CHAPTER II
The Silent Giant

It was still daylight when I got off the train.

I first busied myself with finding a bed for the night; I eventually settled on the Star Hotel, located near the harbor. There, after a brief toilet, I went down to the dining room for an early supper.

The other patrons all belonged to that anonymous throng of travelers who find themselves somewhat lost in a foreign country. They find comfort in groups of folk just like themselves, and take refuge in places that cater to this most transient of crowds.

The Star Hotel was just such a place: it was amorphous, without personality; functional, yet totally devoid of charm.

I knew from experience that a traveler stranded abroad in a foreign city can be exceedingly useful to a good detective. He will be prone to talk to another stranger, quick to yield confidences, without seeking to protect the carefully-built image of himself that he defends at home.

I was pretty certain that at least one of the guests of the Star Hotel would answer my questions without dissimulation or fear of compromising themselves; the only obstacle I had to avoid was the risk of being misled by people all too willing to seem knowledgeable, seeking to impress but, in fact, knowing nothing.

At my right sat a rich merchant, judging by its imposing belly, stuffed inside an expensive white waistcoat that sported a heavy gold chain crossing from one pocket to the other.

As this gentleman looked rather obliging, I selected him to be my first interviewee, and asked if he would pass me a side dish of anchovies. As I had guessed, that proved sufficient to serve as an introduction.

"You are not from Southampton, Mister...?" I began.

"Cooper, Thomas Cooper," he replied. "No, I am of Nottingham, but I come here every month for my business."

"Southampton is an interesting city... There are a number of striking ruins dating back to the Roman era, and, of course, fine medieval buildings like Netley Abbey and the Bargate..."

"Yes, yes, of course, but you see, I have very little time to see the sights when I come down here... Checking in on my clients and taking their orders is all that really interests me..."

"Ah! You are a real businessman..."

"I'd like to think so, and, to speak frankly, I think that a two or three hundred pound order is well worth all the monuments of the world."

"Spoken wisely indeed," I agreed, pouring him a glass of stout. "I have a mind for business myself... I'm an American... You can probably tell from my accent..."

"I was just about to comment on that," my rotund table neighbor replied.

"I just arrived from New York... The crossing was perfect... no incidents... No, excuse me, I'm wrong... We almost sank a three-mast around the Isle of Wight... a ship called, if I remember correctly, the *Matilda Briggs*."

Suddenly, another man, who had been sitting to my left, and had ignored us so far, jumped in and said, looking at me, surprised:

"What did you just say, sir? The *Matilda Briggs* was nearly hit?"

"Why, yes—by the ship on which I was."

"The *Columbia*?"

"Yes."

"I am sorry to hear this, sir—sorry, and grateful. You see, I'm a marine insurance agent, sir, but the captain of the *Matilda Briggs*, who should have reported the incident, said nothing about it... A man normally so careful... Yes, this was the first thing he should have done on arrival."

"I see! So the *Matilda Briggs* is docked in Southampton?"

"Didn't you know it?"

"No. To tell the truth, I thought that, when we encountered her, she was heading south."

"I would very much like to know more, sir, but thank you for what you have just told me... It will go in my report."

I had spun a yarn a little more far-fetched than I had intended, and I hastened to divert the conversation, but the marine insurance agent always brought it back to the *Matilda Briggs*. He now demanded numerous clarifications and consigned inside a notebook the many imaginary details which I gave him with the most serious air in the world.

It was, however, necessary to cut short the interview, which could otherwise upset the port authorities of Southampton and bring unwanted attention upon myself. So I took leave of my fellow diners and went up to my room in order to plan my next move.

My strategy was soon mapped out, for I am one who decides quickly, especially in critical circumstances. I rang the bellboy, who arrived immediately.

"I'm expecting the visit of a friend," I said, "a merchant sailor, a youngish man, about my size... If he asks for me at the reception, please show him to my room, will you?"

"Of course, sir."

"Except for him, I do not want to see anyone else, is that understood?"

"Very well, sir."

After the bellboy had gone, I slipped quietly out of my room, because I had, as we shall see, some serious reasons to not attract the attention of the staff.

I finally made it to the street without encountering a soul.

Once outside, I walked towards the harbor and looked for the type of sordid back alley where I knew I would find what I was looking for.

I eventually located a small shop, with rags hanging outside. I entered and met the owner, an old man with a bald head who looked a little like a vulture.

"I need a complete sailor outfit," I said. "Used... the dingier, the better... It's because of a bet I lost..."

"I certainly have what you seek, sir," replied the man. "Here... this jacket and this pair of pants look like they're your size... As for the hat, you have a choice: do you prefer a cap or a bonnet?"

"A cap, I think."

"Very well... Here is one that is almost new, sir... See, the fabric has not lost its shine... as to the visor, which is slightly damaged, I'll replace it immediately... It'll be only a matter of a minute or so..."

I paid the man ten shillings and six pence, and felt perfectly satisfied with my purchase.

The shopkeeper carefully wrapped the clothes and I returned at once to the Star-Hotel.

Fortunately, the bellboy was not standing in his usual place, which is to say on the ground floor next to the elevator, so I was able to slip in quickly and go back into my room unnoticed. There, I proceeded to transform myself, using the makeup tools that never left me: a reddish beard, adding some rouge to the nose and cheekbones, and a couple of warts. Then, I donned the sailor suit and went out.

Now, I had to face the bellboy and test my disguise. I took the stairs to go down and went looking for him. I took care to look out of place, and walk with that awkward gait that is often characteristic of sailors on dry land.

When the bellboy spotted me, he approached me at once, and inquired as to my business.

"My name's John Evans," I replied in a strong Welsh accent. "I'm a guest of Mr. Dickson."

"Ah, yes," said the bellboy. "He told me about you. I'll take you to his room. Please follow me."

"You are very kind, sir, but in fact, I just come from there."

"Huh? You do? Well, what do you want then?"

"I got a bit lost in here. Could you please direct me to the exit, if you don't mind?"

"Take a right. Make a left at the front desk, then it's in front of you," replied the bellboy, rather gruffly.

"Much obliged, sir!"

And I went away, dragging my feet and swinging from left to right, like sailors do.

My experiment had been a success. The bellboy had not recognized me; I could therefore face the crowds without fear of being identified later.

Once outside, I continued towards the harbor, sill doing my "sailor walk."

It was then 9 p.m.

After walking down High Street and entering the harbor district, I found myself in a small, dimly lit street, and spotted the glowing reflection on the wet sidewalk of the front window of a tavern that appeared to be full of sailors from all around the world.

Without hesitation, I went into this den of iniquity that reeked of the combined smells of sweat, cheap alcohol and pipe tobacco. I've made a practice of being thoroughly acquainted with all kinds of places like this, so I found myself at ease instantly.

My plan was to make friends with the patrons until—and that was the real challenge!—I could find a sailor that belonged to the crew of the *Matilda Briggs*.

It took me just about two hours, and no less than eight pitchers of ale, but I finally found the man I had been looking for all night: he was an ugly Irish runt with a pockmarked face who went by the name of Mr. Pump.

He was already half drunk when I was introduced to him by a burly Welshman and I set about to make him even drunker.

We soon became best friends, and I began to realize that this awful drunkard was, in fact, not a bad man at all, although you would never have guessed it, judging by his looks.

After my new "friend" had polished off the last pitcher of ale, he muttered in a quivering voice:

"You look like you're in funds, Evans... Why, you haven't even chipped your purse yet! Well! As sure as my name's Pump, I would be eternally grateful to you if you were to order a bottle of whiskey. I feel it would put me right, because I've been getting a pasty mouth from that stinking ale they serve here... I'll make it up to you, pal... I swear, when I get paid, I'll treat you like a king... I'm no cad... I wear my heart on my sleeves... We're all like that on the good ol' *Matilda Briggs*... Generous to a fault..."

"She's a steamer?"

"A steamer? Never in my life! No, she's good boat... a small three-mast... goes her eight knots easy, leaving many two pipers in her wake..."

Until now, I hadn't been totally sure that Pump actually served on the *Matilda Briggs*. Now, I was certain.

I immediately ordered a bottle of whisky in the hope of eliciting more information.

"The *Matilda Briggs*, you say?" I said. "I think I know her... We met her at sea once... I think it was around Colombo..."

"It's possible... but not this year, for sure, because we've only been to Ireland and Norway... Before that, I can't say... I used to be aboard the *Pelican*, an old rat-infested brick that was leaking everywhere... Ah! Not like the *Matilda Briggs*! She's a proud ship, mark my words! Not at all young, true, but with that new coat of paint she just got, she looks like a new boat, and you'd swear she's come straight out of the yards at Chatham..."

"How many of you are on board?"

"Thirty-four, including the two cabin boys... no more, no less... Cheers, mate! Golly! This sure is good whiskey, as our captain would say..."

One by one, the sailors left the tavern, and soon, I remained alone with Mr. Pump who, unsurprisingly, was having difficulties marshaling his thoughts.

"I think I'm done for the night, old boy," he stammered. "I have my full load... Oh, yes! For sure, that I have... and I'd do it again!"

And he began to hum that refrain well known to all English sailors in a falsetto voice:

To lie away in a howling breeze
May tickle a landsman's taste;
That goal was the happiest hour sailor sees
Is when he's a clown in a seaport town
With his Nancy on his knee,
And his arm around her waist...

But his sentimental ballad was soon cut off by a sudden attack of hiccups. Pump's head drooped, his eyes became glassy, he leaned back and a loud snoring sound came out of his open mouth.

Hastily, I fumbled through his pockets, snatched up a dirty wallet and promptly paid the tavern keeper, saying:

"I don't think my friend can return to his ship tonight..."

The man looked at the clock and said:

"I'm used to this. Leave him here. At midnight, I'll drop him off on the sidewalk outside. The fresh air will wake him up..."

"Or the police?"

"Could be," replied the tavern keeper unfazed. "It wouldn't be the first time. Well then, he'll spend the night at the station... It might be what's best for him."

Poor Mr. Pump! Yet, I could not very well take him with me to the Star Hotel!

Fifteen minutes later, I was lying in my good, soft bed and soon fell asleep, quite tired of this emotional day, coming right on the heels of my Atlantic crossing.

Tuesday, June 7th

The next day, I arose at sunrise. Shortly before 8 a.m., I left the hotel, wearing the sailor garb that had become familiar to the staff, and I returned to the harbor where I had no trouble finding the *Matilda Briggs*.

She was indeed a very beautiful ship, and I took my time examining her, hoping to attract the attention of one of her crew.

Indeed, it didn't take long before two men stepped off the bridge and came towards me.

"Do you have a man named Pump on your crew?" I inquired.

"Yes," replied the sailor. "He got kicked out of the police station drunk as a skunk barely an hour ago... What do you want from him?"

"That's kind of personal... Could I see him?"

"Oh, you sure can! But he isn't in a state to talk to anyone right now..."

"That's okay."

"Well, then, follow me..."

And that's how I was invited aboard the *Matilda Briggs*.

In the steerage, I found my drunk Irishman. The other sailor had not exaggerated; it was impossible to get a word out of Pump.

I decided to show the wallet to the sailor who had accompanied me and still stood in the corridor.

"That's a shame," I said, "because I have something to give him. I believe it's his; it has his name—Pump—inside."

The sailor looked at the wallet.

"Yes," he said. "I recognize it. It's his wallet indeed. He must have lost it during his drunken binge last night. You can leave it with me, if you want. I'm the Second Mate. I'll give it back to him when he's back in shape."

"Er... I suppose that would be fine," I said, handing him the wallet. "You strike me as a decent sort of fellow."

My interlocutor looked honest and rather talkative. From his accent, I perceived he was a Scotsman, and everyone knows that the people of the far north of England, are, by a strange mystery of nature, as verbose as those from the South of France!

I resolved to take advantage of this meeting to befriend him and learn as much as I could about the *Matilda Briggs*.

"My name is Evans, by the way," I added, extending my hand.

He shook it and replied:

"McDermott. Glad to meet an honest man, Mr. Evans. What ship do you hail from?"

"The *Dundee*."

"I don't think I know her... Is she a sailboat?"

"No. A steamer."

McDermott made a disdainful pout, same as Pump, and then said:

"I don't know your *Dundee*, but I'm sure she's not nearly as fine as our *Matilda Briggs*."

"I'm not so sure."

"Would you like to see her for yourself?"

"By my faith, I sure would! I've always wondered about tugboats like this..."

"Tugboats! I'll show you our *Matilda* is no tugboat," muttered McDermott. "She's worth ten times your sooty dampers."

"So you say!"

"Oh! Of course, you're all the same, on your floating coal piles... Come with me and you'll see that the *Matilda Briggs* is like a palace next to your... er, what is she called, already, your ship?"

"The *Dundee*."

"Yes... The *Dundee*."

I followed McDermott as he gave me a tour of the *Matilda Briggs* and I gradually praised her to high heavens and took back all my previous prejudices against sailboats.

"Well, well... It does look very comfortable," I said, widening his eyes. "And look at this... Really... I never expected..."

"Ah! You see! I told you," said my happy Scotsman.

We visited the front and the back of the ship, and the steerage, and everywhere I found the same mixed smell of brine and tar that is characteristic of a well-maintained schooner.

I made a point to memorize the faces of the other sailors I saw shuffling here and there on their bare feet, but nothing caught my attention.

However, as we reached the end of the crew's quarters, I couldn't help but repress a shudder.

Alone, in a corner, sitting on the floor, leaning against a wall, a man appeared to be sleeping.

Yet, he wasn't truly asleep, because as he heard us approach, he turned his big, black eyes towards us.

He was huge.

His shoulders, packed inside a wide-collared sailor's shirt that only accentuated their breadth, were those of a fairground Hercules. His legs were like tree trunks threatening to burst the seams of his blue serge pants. His arms were hanging between his knees, on either side of his body like two monumental towers; each of his hands was larger than an average dinner plate.

One felt that this Hercules, with those hands, could easily have crushed a woman's body.

I instantly thought of the terrible condition of the corpse I had seen the day before, spread out on the commons at Lyndhurst.

Suddenly, my eyes caught a glimpse of something that sent a shiver down my spine.

Blood! It was not a product of my overheated imagination, but a sinister vision that had arisen before my eyes.

The giant, with a sudden gesture, had just lifted one of his great hands, perhaps to wave us away. The underside of his wrist and the base of his palm had been revealed.

And they were raw, purple—bloody.

With his other hand, the man reached in his pocket for a large handkerchief, yellow with blue squares, marked with large scarlet spots, and, paying us no attention, began to staunch the blood from his wounds. Then, he replaced the handkerchief and returned to his previous silent posture.

I tried to feel calm before that creature who might well be an unspeakably cruel monster with a human face; I knew that a great detective must always be wary of sudden flights of imagination, but there had been so much horror and cruelty in the Lyndhurst murder that not to feel upset at being presented with such a sight would have been inhuman.

I focused my eyes on the mouth of the silent giant.

It was huge and thick-lipped; his square jaws rested on the monstrous trestle of his clavicles and, despite my efforts, that picture evoked in my mind the image of a woman's frail fingers being cracked in that vise like so many hazelnuts.

McDermott dragged me back onto the deck.

"That's quite a guy, our Bill Sharper, huh?" he said. "I'd bet you've never seen one like him on a steamer? But don't let him bother you. He's a good guy, who wouldn't harm a fly... Of course, one shouldn't bother him. He doesn't like company and just wants to be left alone..."

Brutal, brooding, silent... Had I at last found the monster? Deep passions may sometimes fester in solitude, and suddenly be transformed into unprecedented explosions of savagery...

And then, there was his bloodied handkerchief...

I had to be careful to not let my imagination run wild and reach an all too obvious conclusion. Logic, and nothing else, must dictate my actions.

"What did you say his name was?" I asked McDermott.

"Bill Sharper," he replied. "He's a good man, who doesn't like to be disturbed."

"Is he always... like this?"

"Always. Lost in his thoughts. It's his way of passing the time."

"Maybe he's drunk?" I suggested.

"Sharper? No, no one on board has ever seen him drunk. I, for one, have never seen him take even a single drink. He's like a camel in that respect. Besides, he never leaves the ship."

"He doesn't?"

"No more than he drinks, laughs, or talks."

"Is he a good sailor?"

"The best. He keeps the ship tidy and clean. You should see him at the roll call... Always spick and span, shining like a new penny."

"Really?"

"Yes. You would never believe it, from a man like him."

"I noticed he's hurt..."

"Oh! It's nothing. He probably scratched his hand against a nail when he was polishing the deck... because he scrubs it hard when he puts his mind to it."

"Is he English?"

"I'm not sure. Sometimes, I think he's a Scot like me, and you wouldn't believe me if I told you that he cries like a little girl when I sing ballads from my country."

I told myself that an emotional display of sensitivity in an otherwise brooding fellow could be a sign of mental unbalance. But one thing bothered me and virtually negated all the other clues: I'd just been told that Sharper never went ashore! And I didn't believe he was the type of man whose absence would not have been immediately noticed.

"Why," I asked bluntly, "does he never go ashore?"

"How should I know? Perhaps it makes him feel sad... Brings back old memories, bad ones..."

"An old romance perhaps?"

"Bill Sharper? Women? Certainly not! I swear that's not what keeps him awake at night!"

As there was nothing more to find out, I decided to abandon this line of inquiry, but still felt troubled by Sharper's taste for isolation, which, in my opinion, is often a symptom of other mental problems.

I returned to the topic of the respective merits of three-masted schooners versus steam-powered ships and

McDermott was all too thrilled to again brag about the merits of his *Matilda Briggs*.

Thanks to my stratagem, I had gained entry aboard the ship, identified a possible suspect, and now I found myself in possession of a trove of new information to be presented to Sherlock Holmes' sagacity.

It was time for me to leave and report on my mission. McDermott told me that the *Matilda Briggs* would not set sail for another five days. That left us plenty of time to assess the situation and take action, if needed.

I agreed with good grace that schooners were indeed superior to steamers and took leave of my obliging cicerone.

For the third time, the now-familiar sailor John Evans went to visit Harry Dickson at the Star Hotel, but never came out. Instead, half an hour later, Harry Dickson himself, now shaved, washed, powdered and perfumed, went down to have lunch.

I cabled Sherlock Holmes that I would see him for dinner that same evening.

At 2:30 p.m., I took the train to London.

CHAPTER III
The Man in Grey

Baker Street was unusually quiet when I arrived. The red brick houses and their identical windows stood a silent watch. I knew Holmes' residence well as I had visited him before.

221B was, by then, one of the world' s most recognized addresses and its description was regularly featured in magazine columns across the globe.

During the journey, I had mulled over the mystery of the *Matilda Briggs* and her mysterious sailor, Bill Sharper, without coming any closer to figuring out what seemed to be an insoluble problem of staggering proportions.

I rang the bell. Almost immediately, I heard the muffled sound of footsteps inside. The bronze green painted oak door opened and Mrs. Hudson appeared, bent by age.

I was going to identify myself, but obviously Holmes must have left instructions because, before I could utter a word, she said:

"Mr. Holmes is waiting for you."

So I went in and up the stairs.

In his chambers, so often and well described by Dr. Watson, Sherlock Holmes sat in a checkered black and white dressing gown, a pipe in his mouth, his eyes closed, thinking. On a nearby table, I couldn't help but notice the presence of a Pravaz syringe.

At first, it seemed as if he had not noticed me enter, but suddenly, he opened his eyes and uttered these words:

"So it was the *Matilda Briggs* in Southampton, was it not, Harry?"

"You knew, sir?"

"No, I merely suspected, as I came here straight from Lyndhurst. However, when I didn't see you return from Southampton last night, I assumed you had indeed found the *Matilda Briggs*."

I tried to excuse myself for not cabling him a report, but Holmes waved my words away with a gesture of his hand.

"No need to apologize. You did well, Harry. And judging from your expression, you must have found a trail? But you don't know what it means; you only suspect, otherwise you'd have cabled me earlier. Out with it, young man. What is it that you found?"

Once again, I couldn't but admire his quick, penetrating intelligence. I nodded and told him of my visit aboard the *Matilda Briggs*.

"That sailor... Bill Sharper... Have you talked to him?" he asked after I was finished.

"No," I replied. "He seems to speak to no one."

"A lonely, silent man... Do you think he could be our Jack the Ripper?" asked Holmes, staring at me.

"Well, to be honest, I don't know yet, sir. It is true that this Sharper fellow seems to be the type that we're looking for... He fits the picture of a monstrously strong murderer who repeats the same crimes whenever his ship reaches a harbor..."

"Be more precise. What makes you suspect him?"

"His gigantic size denotes unusual strength; his brutish behavior and his sense of isolation might be clues of murderous tendencies..."

"Yes, but these are mere appearances, Harry, and a true detective should never rely on just appearances... You had already conjured up a preconceived portrait of our murderer before you even climbed aboard the *Matilda Briggs*, and when you saw Bill Sharper, a man of the type that matched your mental image, you immediately told yourself: 'here is our man!'"

I confessed that he wasn't wrong; I had indeed created a picture of our killer in my mind before I set foot on the ship.

"I'm partially responsible for this," continued Holmes, "because I set you on the wrong track... The *Matilda Briggs* is important to our case, but not in the way you think. During your absence, I have gathered other important evidence that leads me to think that our killer is not part of her crew."

"You know this for a fact?" I asked, astounded.

"Yes, I do. I even have a witness."

I became confused.

"But why do you believe our man couldn't be Bill Sharper?"

"Because of his uniform, Harry."

"His uniform?"

Holmes shook his pipe in the ashtray, then continued:

"You described his clothes: the white shirt, the blue serge pants... Not a trace of blood on them. Killers of the type we're pursuing are violent lunatics; they never commit their crimes in cold blood; they're not calculating; they're blinded by a sudden blood lust. Rage overpowers them, and they must kill. To a sailor, his uniform is like a second skin. A man like Bill Sharper would never dream of taking the precaution of removing it beforehand and storing it safely before committing such a foul, violent murder. If he had killed in a fit of madness, his clothes would have been drenched in blood... Hiding behind a disguise implies a lucidity and deviousness that is incompatible with the signs of temporary madness we beheld."

Holmes' statement made sense and challenged all my previous assumptions. So I asked hesitantly:

"So the murderer is someone else?"

"Indeed. As it turned out, he was spotted by a woman. You see, I noticed that the pathologist had made an error and that death occurred earlier in the morning—at dawn, to be precise... So I expanded the search for witnesses and located a woman who actually saw the murderer—rather vaguely, true, but still... The killer was a man wearing a gray coat. But I want you to listen to her by yourself..."

So saying, Holmes pressed a bell.

"Mrs. Hudson, could you please bring Mrs. Porter back in?" he asked. "Anticipating your return," he continued, talking to me, "I asked the lady to wait. She is now so afraid of encountering that monster again that she was all too happy to stay here under my protection."

Mrs. Porter entered. She was an ordinary, country woman, neat, plump, with perhaps a hint of a mustache over her upper lip. She looked to be thirty to thirty-five years-old. Nothing about her indicated that she might be one of those neurotic attention-seekers that one encounters all too often in the detective business.

She appeared to be the wife of a shopkeeper, or perhaps an artisan, but the gold chain that adorned her bodice betrayed financial well-being.

Holmes invited her to sit.

"Mrs. Porter," he said, "this is Harry Dickson, my associate... My protégé... I would like you to gather your memories again and tell him what you told me earlier."

"Oh, sir!" she suddenly began, her expression changing to one of true terror. "What I saw was awful... yes, truly awful... As long as I live, I'll never forget this dreadful spectacle!"

"Please speak, and leave no details out," urged Holmes.

"Yes, sir... yes, I understand... let me explain... but, I'm sorry... I'm so confused... Here's what happened... First, I must tell you that we are gardeners; every morning, my husband and I bring vegetables to the market in Southampton. When we drove by the commons at Lyndhurst, something disturbed our mare. My husband went down to see what it was and I came to his aid. It wasn't quite daybreak yet; you could barely see twenty steps ahead. Suddenly, I heard a cry for help and there, on the commons, deserted at this time as you may well suppose, I saw, perhaps ten yards away, a woman running. I thought I recognized one of my neighbors, a young woman named Betty Beaton who sometimes takes advantage of our cart to come with us to the market. I had the notion then that Betty had gotten off to a late start and, wanting to catch up with us, had taken a short-cut through the fields behind our house. So I called to her: 'Betty! Betty!' I shouted.

"I did not understand a word of what she was screaming about, but suddenly, I felt that she was in danger. Our old mare had become frightened, too. So I told my husband, 'Stay here; I'll go and see what's going on. It's Betty Beaton. It must be important.' And so I ran onto the commons... Then, I heard more cries from the unfortunate girl... my husband heard them too... She was begging for help in a voice that I will never forget. 'For the love of God, help me!' she shouted. 'He is after me! Please help!'"

Here, Mrs. Porter stopped, breathless at the memory of that tragic night.

I looked at Holmes. Wordlessly, he signaled me to wait. I nodded and bit my lips in frustration.

After regaining her composure, Mrs. Porter continued:

"Ah! Gentlemen, what an awful thing I saw... I was already fairly close to Betty and I knew I was going catch up with her when *something* passed me... It struck me, or pushed me aside, because I found myself falling backwards into the hedge that separates the commons from the tennis court, but I soon recovered... I could see the man who'd just passed me... his huge back... his thick legs... He wore no hat, at least that I noticed, and he was dressed all in gray. I saw all this in a blur, gentlemen, but these details remain fixed in my mind... Then, I heard screams, terrible screams, excruciating screams, agonizing screams... the screams of someone being murdered... savagely... with great ferocity... Then... Then, I don't know... My husband at first hadn't dared leave our cart, for fear the horse would run off, but when he heard the screams, he rushed to my rescue, shouting all the way to scare away the monster.

"I can't tell you what that murderer did to our neighbor... because it was her, yes, it was indeed our Betty... I'd recognized her right away, poor Betty... She always wore a purple dress and the awful corpse I saw on the commons wore a dress of that same color. I think that, at that moment, I fainted... All I remember is that, when I came to, I was back in our cart alongside my husband and we were driving toward Southampton.

"I asked him what had happened, and he replied: "Tis an awful thing, but we can't change anything to what happened to that poor woman, and people like us should not meddle in matters of concern to the police... 'Tis best to be quiet and say nothing.'"

Holmes shrugged with a wry smile. Mrs. Porter continued:

"I assure you that, upon our return from Southampton, I felt great remorse; but my husband still told me: 'Shut up! We can't change anything to what happened!' But I couldn't stand it, Gentlemen. As soon as I found out from my neighbors that Mr. Sherlock Holmes himself was investigating the matter, I made up an excuse and took the first train to London and came to see you... I don't think I'll be able to sleep, not until I see the murderer of our poor Betty climb the steps to the gallows!"

Mrs. Porter finally fell silent.

It was obvious that this woman had seen something, but her fear might still influence her recollection.

"Are you certain, Madam, that the man you saw was dressed all in gray?" I asked. "As you said yourself, you'd just fallen and, in the morning mist, you might have..."

But Mrs. Porter protested:

"I'm sorry to interrupt, sir, but there was no fog that morning. Yes, it wasn't quite daylight yet, but I could already see colors quite clearly."

"So the murderer was wearing a gray coat?"

"Yes, iron gray."

"But no hat?"

"Indeed. But he could easily have lost it on his way, because he was running like a madman, sir... and he was breathing hard, I heard it... It sounded like he had a bellows inside his throat. I did not see his face, but his head, from what I could see from behind, seemed... enormous..."

"What do you mean?"

"It was gigantic... Bigger even than that of Reverend Patterson's, our pastor, who has a fairly large head."

Sherlock Holmes rose.

"Thank you, Madam," he said. "That's all we needed to know. We will have to question your husband... Just tell him that it's necessary, absolutely necessary, but rest assured that you will incur no trouble whatsoever... In fact, I'd like you to continue to remain silent on the matter, not to speak of it to your neighbors, and especially not to your local constabulary. I will take care of everything."

"I know your reputation, Mr. Holmes," replied the woman. "But I confess I'm a bit afraid to return to Lyndhurst."

"Are you concerned that your husband might reproach you?"

"Well, yes, a little, but mostly, I fear... the man in gray."

"Don't. Go home quickly, don't go out unaccompanied at night, and you should be safe."

The unfortunate woman hesitated and watched us both with pleading eyes, but Holmes was not moved.

"Come... Goodbye, Madam... Or you risk missing the last train back to Lyndhurst. But I will come and see you very soon..."

Mrs. Porter got up reluctantly and one could feel the fear that gripped her at the thought of returning to the scene of that awful crime.

After she had gone, Holmes came to stand in front of me.

"So, what do you think, Harry?" he asked. "I assume you have no objections to keeping the police in the dark for the time being?"

"None whatsoever," I replied. "Now, what do I think? A man in gray, yes... Her evidence seems undeniable... Yet, the brutish figure I saw aboard the *Matilda Briggs* still haunts me, Mr. Holmes... There are no two beings like him in England, capable of such strength... such savagery..."

"I wish you'd let that drop for the moment," Holmes said rather peremptorily. "We must follow the trail offered to us by this woman."

"You believe that it will lead us to the killer?"

"Yes, I do, Harry. But it is essential to obtain the testimony of her husband. So we will return to Lyndhurst tomorrow—before Her Majesty's police have had the time to muck it up..."

Holmes then returned to his seat, raised his sleeve, carefully pulled up the wrist of his shirt, grabbed the syringe and proceeded to inject himself in the arm with a small dose of morphine. Then, he leaned back in his chair, blew three rings of smoke with his pipe and closed his eyes.

"There's nothing more to be learned from the examination of the victim's body," he muttered. "We know her name and her home. She did not know her attacker. It was indeed a crime of madness, one of those periodic, sadistic murders... Our research must be confined to the insane... That's a step in the right direction... After that..."

He made a vague gesture in my direction, which may have been his way of waving me good-bye.

"I will see you tomorrow at the Southampton station at 9 a.m. sharp," I said.

I took my hat and shook his hand.

"Tomorrow at nine," I repeated.

Holmes did not rise to see me out, which was a touching mark of familiarity on the part of this great man.

CHAPTER IV
Growing Suspicions

In the train back to Southampton, I reviewed the events of the day, as was my practice.

Holmes' attitude puzzled me greatly. First, he had sent me looking for the *Matilda Briggs*, suggesting that the murderer might belong to her crew, outlining the periodic visits of the ship to England and the bloody trail she seemed to leave behind her.

I had acted upon that information, and believed that I had found the thread that might eventually lead to solving the mystery of this new Jack the Ripper.

But now, Holmes, not paying attention to the clues I'd found, had instead launched himself on a new trail, based purely on the assertions of a simple village woman.

That was puzzling, to say the least

When we arrived at the station, I was more than ever convinced that my mentor knew far more than he had hinted and was purposefully hiding things from me; what I didn't know was what and why, but I resolved to find out.

Since we had arranged to meet the next day at the railway station at 9 a.m., I had the entire evening free to see if I could dig up something more incriminating regarding the *Matilda Briggs* in general, and the mysterious Bill Sharper in particular.

I decided to again dress up as Evans, the sailor from the *Dundee*, and return to the tavern where I had first met Mr. Pump, the Irish sailor whose wallet I had stolen.

I returned to my hotel and, in a jiffy, changed outfits. As luck would have it, it was a busy night and no one paid any attention to either me or the disreputable-looking sailor who left my room a few minutes later.

I reached the docks, but moved by a sudden inspiration, I changed my mind. Instead of going to the tavern, I decided to keep an eye on the *Matilda Briggs*.

I had no plausible excuse for boarding her again, so I merely hid behind a pile of crates and waited.

Soon, night fell, and it became very dark. Eventually, a sailor raised the gangplank and took down the lantern, a sure sign that they expected no one to either leave or come aboard. Had my wait been in vain?

I began pacing the docks, staring at the pavement, lit by a single gas lamp near the semaphore at the end of the pier. Ten o'clock struck. I saw a group of sailors walk by, but they were from the *Atlantic* and the *Grosvenor*—none belonged to the *Matilda Briggs*.

Then, even sailors became scarce. The night had gone deathly quiet.

Suddenly, I froze, for I had just heard a suspicious noise coming from the *Matilda Briggs*. Had someone spotted me?

I rushed back to hide behind the crates and looked up.

Above the railing, a pair of legs had appeared; they dropped down, and I saw a man clinging with both hands to one of the chains that held the boat to the dock

The silhouette slid along the chain with such agility that I could scarcely restrain a cry of amazement.

Despite the darkness, I could tell that the man who had just come down from the *Matilda Briggs* was gigantic.

"Sharper! Bill Sharper!" I said to myself. "And I was told he never went ashore!"

I was suddenly tempted to grab this man, but a flash of reason stopped me. What use would it be to struggle with such a colossus? And even if I succeeded in disabling him, what would it prove, except that he took unauthorized leave?

So I stood silent and motionless and let Sharper set foot on the docks.

He passed me barely a few feet away, but did not notice my presence behind the crates, as I crouched in the dark.

I began to follow him. My right hand, safely inside my pocket, rested on my Browning.

The sailor walked rapidly, with long strides, making it difficult to follow him without being noticed. I wondered if it was the madness of the murderer that added to his already considerable strength.

We crossed through half-a-dozen dark alleys, where the songs of drunk sailors echoed against the grimy walls.

I did not know Southampton well and, in the dark, I was even less able to identify the path that Sharper took through its maze of narrow streets.

Despite the harrowing pace that he set, I continued my train of thoughts. Whoever was rushing ahead of me had to be the murderer... The new Jack the Ripper... So my suspicions were correct! This madman had cleverly convinced his fellow crew that he never went ashore, when the truth was otherwise.

As he walked under a street lamp, I shuddered because, for the first time, I was able to take a look at him, and realized that the man I was following was *wearing a gray coat*!

In my mind, the solution to the murders was no longer in question.

I was almost out of breath, but I continued to follow the huge man, never losing sight of his swaying silhouette. I shivered, not knowing if it was caused by the horror of the discovery, or the joy of being proven right.

I realized that we had been walking for a good while, and were now on the outskirts of town. Only a few passersby crossed our path; lonely figures at that hour of the night.

When they passed Sharper, I saw them turn their heads in his direction, so surprised were they by his unusual size. If only these peaceful people had known the awful truth!

We finally reached a small square surrounded by a row of brick houses, as one usually finds in the suburbs of most British towns. The houses were low, narrow, without any style or decoration; they were the homes of workers or artisans; many had adjacent sheds.

I saw a few trees—acacias—arranged clumsily around the square; gas lamps flickered at each corner; one was off, leaving that entire corner in darkness.

My giant moved towards that dark area. I became afraid to lose sight of him, and although I was quite out of breath, I began to run on tiptoes to get closer to him.

Fortunately, he turned into another well-lit road that started at the corner of the square. It ran towards the outside of town; its streetlights were all functioning and provided pale rectangles of light at regular intervals. It was bordered on both sides by rows of gray brick walls—warehouses, small factories and the like. There were fewer houses.

Suddenly, my heart began to beat wildly.

In one of the lit spaces, a figure loomed, moving in and out of the shadows. It was a woman!

She left the lit area and plunged into the darkness, but I had seen the direction which she took... She was coming towards us... Indeed, her silhouette reappeared in a box of light only a few steps away from Bill Sharper.

A sudden fright seized me at the sight of this fragile woman next to that awful monster. I stood frozen on the spot, helpless, as if I'd been watching two trains rushing at full speed towards each other.

I grabbed my revolver.

The man in gray stopped. I saw him put his hand in his pocket, pull out his handkerchief and wipe his brow.

Had he seen the woman?

She was now approaching him, unsuspecting. Should I stop her? Shout with all the strength of my lungs, "Save yourself!"

But it might only precipitate an attack.

Being there, I could intervene at the risk of my own life, if the madman decided to jump on his prey. I knew I would only have one chance to smash the murderer's head before he would get the better of me.

This would destroy Holmes' and my own careful investigation, but I couldn't abandon this poor woman to the terrible fate that might await her. How could I remain an impassive witness to her terrible slaughter?

All this took less than a second. I moved forward...

The woman was now only steps away from the brute...

I felt a deadly chill creep up along my legs. I instinctively pointed my weapon toward the giant...

The woman approached him...

I saw the monster stop and lean towards her; then I caught a few whispered words. The heavy man's shoulders rose in a gesture that expressed disdain, then he continued on his way, while the woman walked towards me.

I let out a breath which I could have sworn I had been holding for a good time.

Never, I said to myself, *will this unfortunate woman suspect the danger in which she was.*

When she approached me, I understood at once what kind of indecent proposal she had made to the giant.

I turned her down, but I could have kissed her, so happy I was to see her out of danger!

Bill Sharper was now back in the lead. We were on the outskirts of Southampton. Even the factories had given way to fields and hedges. In the distance, I heard a clock chime midnight.

The countryside was lit only by the stars above, for the night was moonless.

I never lost sight of the sailor. He eventually stopped before a lonely house with a chalky white plaster facade, surrounded by hedges. I hid behind a tree. I saw him looking around a couple of times, then I heard him knock on the door, several times, according to what sounded like a pre-set pattern.

Everything fell silent.

When I looked again, the man in gray had disappeared.

CHAPTER V
The Mysterious House

Wednesday, June 8th

In the past, young noblemen spent a night in prayer and meditation before being knighted and called it a "white night."

This was their final test, the one that made them worthy of belonging to an order of warriors without fear or reproach.

I imagine that it was very much a night like that which I passed outside that little white house in the outskirts of Southampton, and perhaps it was just as necessary in order for me to earn the honor of being called a detective.

Bill Sharper had momentarily evaded me, but I knew he was inside that house. Yet for what sinister purpose? For what monstrous gratifications of his unholy passions?

I was waiting for him to come out to arrest him. No doubt, I would find plenty of evidence inside.

The capture of one of the most dreadful criminals that England had ever known was something I relished.

I was sweating despite the cold of the night and it was as if an icy shroud had fallen onto my shoulders. I paced back and forth on the road to fight the cold. But even that ultimately proved futile.

Eventually I could no longer stand it and had to sit down in a ditch on the side of the road, opposite the house, and wrap myself in old newspapers, like a tramp.

That bone-white facade, shining under the cold light of the stars in the darkness, hypnotized me. I did not take my eyes off it. But I detected no beam of light between the cracks in the shutters, nor heard the slightest echo of voices from the inside. In short, there were none of those thousand small clues that indicate the presence of living beings inside a house.

I looked at my watch—a wonderful timepiece from Switzerland—and saw that it was almost 2 a.m.

"Another four hours till sunrise," I said to myself. "But if Sharper wants to return to the harbor and slip back on the *Matilda Briggs* unnoticed, he'll have to leave at least a couple of hours before that. No way can he keep his nightly excursion a secret if he returns after sunrise..."

I resolved to stay on my watch until something happened. I had gained in confidence and, despite the cold and the fatigue, the thrill of this manhunt helped me stay awake and vigilant.

I was prepared to face two eventualities: Either Bill Sharper would come out, as I hoped, and I would use the element of surprise to jump him and arrest him; it would be a perilous move, seeing that we were alone and he might have accomplices in the mysterious house... Or alternatively, I would leave my watch at dawn.

Either way, I planned to report my adventure to Sherlock Holmes, and reveled in advance at the surprise the great man would feel when I would tell him: "I was right, the killer was Bill Sharper."

I smiled at that thought, happy to have a chance to impress the great detective, whose fame had become universal.

In my fantasy, I had forgotten that pride often comes before the fall...

It was now 5 a.m., and nothing had moved, either inside the house or nearby.

In desperation, I hit upon a fresh idea.

Slowly and carefully, I left my post and went around the house to take a look at the rear. There was an enclosure behind a five foot-tall wall. I approached and found an old crate. Positioning it against the wall, I took a look inside. I discovered a very ordinary garden, with squares of cabbages, rows of vegetables, separated by small straight alleys, intersecting at right angles... There was even some laundry hanging on a wire stretched between two wooden poles.

Nothing in this honest, ordinary decor indicated that that house might be the lair of a gang of criminals.

Now I had to test my hypothesis.

I grabbed my revolver and fired a shot in the air. The sound rang through the night, reverberating on the distant factory buildings. I even smelled the characteristic scent of gunpowder.

Now I was certain that they—whoever *they* might be—had to have heard me from the house. I crouched along the wall, holding my breath.

However, as nothing moved, I grew bolder and took a look.

Where was the horde of villains that should have come out looking for me, or at least scampered away?

More importantly, where was Bill Sharper?

Could he have sniffed me on his trail? Perhaps, he had sensed that he was being spied upon, and had gone into the first, deserted house on this road in order to escape me?

If so, it implied that his crimes were premeditated, planned, organized, and not, as my mentor had postulated, the result of sudden murderous impulses...

This lunatic may not be a madman after all, but a very sly villain.

If he had managed to give me the slip, then it followed that the house must have had at least two exits.

Seeking to test this, and now convinced that the house was empty, I climbed over the wall and took a good look around.

It didn't take me long to find a small, low door in a corner, barely visible from a distance, as its pale color blended in with the white wall. It was made of solid oak, without moldings.

Using my flashlight, I checked the hinges, which appeared rusted. I examined the ground near the door, hoping to find footprints.

There were none!

And yet the earth all around it was wet, due to a recent watering of the garden.

Outside of that door and the front door, there were no other issues, except for a small rectangular opening under the roof, from which a trickle of water fell into in a half bucket clogged with dead leaves.

The house had but two openings, but no clues proved that Sharper had exited through either one. So where was he?

I went back to the road.

It was now almost dawn and, in the distance, I heard the sound of hooves clopping, as farmers were going into town, and workers from the night shift were returning home.

On the horizon, a line of pale light announced the approach of day.

It was nearly 6 a.m.

Then the crowds approached in clusters, passed before me, and, for a minute, I lost sight of the main entrance of the house.

Perhaps Bill Sharper had outwaited me and taken advantage of this confusion to disappear by mingling in with the crowd?

The human tide passed, leaving behind a whiff of sweat and iron.

The sky was now lit up. I had no choice but to give up my watch and return to town.

Now I had but one thing in mind: to call on the captain of the *Matilda Briggs*, identify myself, and arrest Bill Sharper—assuming, of course, that he had somehow managed to return to his ship.

CHAPTER VI
The Sailor Who Never Went Ashore

The return trip to the city seemed endless. When I had gone out the night before, despite the exhaustion resulting from having to follow the man in gray, the excitement generated by the chase, and my hopes for a speedy arrest, had given me enough strength to carry on and kept my spirits high.

Now that I no longer felt that way, I fell prey to a deep weariness.

The sun shone in all its glory when I finally reached the center of Southampton. I had again crossed the square with the stunted acacia trees and seen the opening of shops and workshops where busy artisans and rumbling machines were beginning their day's work.

I had made up my mind to return to the harbor. At some point, a policeman mistook me for a rogue sailor and wanted to take me to his station, so I had to show him my card. He marveled at my disguise and even offered to accompany me aboard the *Matilda Briggs*.

The gangplank was down and, assisted by the helpful bobby, I got on board without difficulty.

Despite the early hour, I was quickly introduced to the Captain of the *Matilda Briggs*, Arthur Beech. He had just finished his toilet and was shaving, but my presence aboard did not seem to faze the old sea dog.

"You're with the police, right?" he asked me gruffly. "So, what do you want? Out with it, boy! By God, I have nothing to fear. Everything on my ship is in order."

I decided to first apologize for my intrusion.

"Yes, Captain," I admitted, "but I'm a private detective..."

"A snitch, then! I don't like snitches!"

I considered it diplomatic to not respond to the insult.

"I'm a private detective," I continued, "and therefore, not part of the police—not quite the same thing. Moreover, my business has nothing to do with your ship, but a member of your crew, a sailor named Bill Sharper..."

The Captain looked at me, surprised.

"It's Sharper you want? Well, yes, he's indeed part of my crew—the best of them, to tell you the truth. There is nothing about him to reproach."

"On board your ship, maybe; but a perfect sailor on this boat may be a totally different man ashore."

Captain Beech shrugged.

"I see what it is now," he says. "Likely a row between drunken sailors in a tavern... Perhaps worse... But you're mistaken, Mr. Private Detective. My Bill Sharper never goes ashore."

"Well..."

"Never, you hear me, by God!"

And the Captain, having finished shaving, plunged his face into his bowl, snorting and throwing water through the mouth and nostrils like a sperm whale.

I finally resumed:

"Bill Sharper spent last night wandering about Southampton."

"I don't believe you!"

"I'm not lying, Captain. It's my job to follow people just as it is yours to captain a ship, and a fellow the size of your Sharper can't be confused with another man."

"But I forbade the whole crew to go ashore last night!"

"I'm not doubting you, because Sharper left the ship in a fashion that was most unusual."

"What do you mean?" asked the Captain, darting his suspicious eyes at me.

"The Bill Sharper I saw leave your ship at 10 p.m. last night, climbed down to the docks surreptitiously and wore a suit."

The assurance with which I delivered this statement finally shook Captain Beech's conviction.

"You say that Sharper went ashore... at 10 p.m.... dressed in some kind of landlubber attire?"

"A proper suit and a coat made of gray cloth, yes, Captain. I watched him, from behind a pile of crates. Your sailor passed only a few feet from me, and I can assure you it was indeed Bill Sharper."

"I'll be... What then?"

"Then I followed your man, because I had very serious motives to do so. He walked through the city but I lost him in the suburbs. He went into a house and disappeared."

"Didn't he come out of that house?"

"Perhaps he did, but if so, I missed him."

"Hum! Hum!" grumbled the Captain. "What you're telling me is unbelievable... Bill Sharper is an excellent sailor and, as I said, he's never gone ashore before... Besides, if he wanted to do it, why do it in secret, instead of asking for permission which, of course, I wouldn't have refused him?"

"Only he can tell us that, Captain."

"Well, I'll ask him, but I warn you, I don't like what you've told me... I have no love for the police, and I don't like it when one of my crew is being treated as suspect..."

The Captain put on his jacket without taking time to button it and pushed me out of his cabin.

"Come with me," he said. "I'll call the men, and you'd better be right..."

We arrived on the bridge where the Captain immediately began to summon his crew.

A moment later, barefoot seamen gathered on the deck, still wet from their morning washing, and lined up shoulder to shoulder. They looked at me with curiosity. In the crowd, I recognized McDermott and my Irish runt, Mr. Pump, who stared at me in amazement.

A quick glance soon convinced me that Bill Sharper was not present. The Captain also noticed it, because he gave me a dirty look.

He then proceeded to do a roll call.

"Sharper? Sharper? Has anyone seen saw Bill Sharper?"

No one answered, but on all sides, this unusual question produced an effect comparable to the announcement of the disappearance, during the night, of the foremast or the main sail.

The Captain then asked in a curt tone:

"Who is Sharper's hammock neighbor?"

A small ginger-haired sailor stepped forward, a red beret in hand:

"I, Captain."

"Has Sharper spent the night in his hammock?"

The little man's shrug said much about the overwhelming power of sleep among exhausted sailors.

"So you don't know if Sharper slept on board last night... Was he at the roll call?"

"Yes, Captain."

"Did you see him go to bed?"

"As I see you now, Captain."

"And after that ?"

"Then I fell asleep, and I thought he had too, Captain."

"Idiot!" growled the annoyed Captain. "Go and check if his things are still here."

The little sailor slipped away, afraid. I was careful not to gloat, for fear of further angering Captain Beech. McDermott, the Second Mate, was furiously chewing his mustache and looked at me from time to time.

"No permissions to go ashore for anyone for the next week!" finally shouted Captain Beech.

Then, fists clenched, he turned towards the young red-haired sailor who had returned from steerage.

"Everything is there, Captain," reported the man. "His bag is still here, with all his clothes in it."

Captain Beech turned towards me:

"Harumph! So he can't be gone for long. Are you satisfied now, Mr. Private Detective?"

"Indeed, I am, Captain. I now know what I wished to know, and it only remains for me to thank you for your great kindness."

The old sea dog coughed and spat furiously as if to expel the anger that still stifled him. Finally, he asked:

"What's your business with Sharper? What did he do?"

I made an evasive gesture:

"Only time might tell, Captain... I can't say anything more for the present... but if you don't mind, when Sharper returns, have him put in irons."

"Eh! By a thousand million portholes!" the Captain burst out. "Do you think I need you to tell me how to enforce discipline on my ship? Now get away, Mr. Private Detective, and don't set foot aboard again unless you want to be thrown into the sea."

I only bowed even more deeply:

"Thank you for your courtesy and your kind welcome, Captain."

I left this inhospitable ship nimbly, considering myself lucky that I was still dry and unharmed, in possession of all my limbs.

"All's well here," I said to myself. "When Sharper returns, that brute of a captain will put him in shackles and it will be easier to wrap up the investigation..."

I made it to my hotel, went up to my room and again exchanged my sailor outfit for the attire of a gentleman.

Sherlock Holmes would be waiting for me at the station at nine. It was eight-thirty and I had no time to waste.

"Tomorrow," I told myself, "all the London newspapers will tell the world that I, Harry Dickson, have just captured the elusive Jack the Ripper!"

CHAPTER VII
The Disappearance of Mrs. Murphy

I was on time to pick up my mentor at the station at 9 a.m., as scheduled. I had hired a cab and, together, we drove up the Porters'.

They lived in a somewhat isolated farm alongside a road lined with hedges, next to a small wood, just outside of town.

Upon our arrival, Mrs. Porter appeared on the threshold to greet us.

"Ah! Gentlemen! You made it!" she said. "I have not slept all night... My husband made a scene when I told him I'd gone to London to talk to the famous Sherlock Holmes!"

"Is Mr. Porter here?' Holmes asked.

"Yes, of course, Mr. Holmes. You'll see him... But you must excuse him; he's a little rough around the edges, and has something of a temper, but basically, he's a good man. Only, he's very much afraid of getting into trouble with the law."

Drawn by the murmur of our conversation, Mr. Porter appeared. He was exactly as I had portrayed him in my mind: surly, unwashed, somewhat loutish with a low forehead and small, piggish eyes filled with mistrust.

"My wife told me about you," he said. "I don't want to be involved in this business. It's not my job to help the police solve crimes. Nothing good will come of it. What do you want from me, anyway? I saw nothing."

Holmes put his hand on the farmer's shoulder in a friendly manner.

"As God is my witness, we are not asking you to report anything but the truth, my good friend. Tell us only what you saw in Lyndhurst that morning. The duty of an honest man is, as you must know, to help as best as he can in the capture of a monster who's terrorizing the whole county."

Porter harrumphed something which could be construed as a sign of acquiescence and stepped aside to let us enter.

It was a clean room that served at once as kitchen, dining room and living room.

"Sit down, gentlemen," said Porter, gesturing towards the table. "I'll tell you one thing: if everyone was like me, concentrating on one's work and not paying attention to other people's business, we wouldn't be talking about monsters and murderers. True, our neighbor Betty Beaton died... It's a crying shame, because she was a good woman, but she was never home. We always saw her on the roads at all hours of the day and night... Myself, I think that when she was surprised by the killer, she wasn't expecting us to drive by on our cart, as my wife believes. She was more likely returning from God knows where..."

Porter didn't finish his sentence. It was clear that, despite what he felt about Miss Beaton's morality, she was dead and, therefore, entitled to some respect.

Holmes insisted:

"But you must have seen something... Heard her screams...?"

"Maybe, but I was busy keeping my mare steady on the road and I cared little about what was happening around us. My wife ran forth, and she told you what she saw, or thinks she saw... Women always exaggerate..."

"But the reality of the murder is proof that Mrs. Porter did not dream what she told us..."

"No, she didn't dream it... But she may not know exactly what it was that she saw... She sees Men in grey everywhere now! For my part, I didn't notice any gray man, and all I ask is to be left in peace..."

"Mr. Porter," I interjected, "you can't possibly live in peace while this terrible monster roams the country-side freely?"

Porter showed us his huge fists.

"By God!" he growled. "Let him come and I'll give him a piece of this!"

I was wondering what my mentor was hoping to find from this interrogation. It seemed to me that neither of the Porters had very much to tell us.

"You said that Miss Beaton often went out at night and returned home in the wee hours of the morning," said Holmes.

Porter harrumphed again, clearly uncomfortable about the subject. I wondered if he himself hadn't enter-tained a liaison at one time or another with the dead girl. Certainly, the good Mrs. Porter showed not the least suspicion about her husband's behavior.

"That is true, Mr. Holmes," she said. "Our Betty was a good girl, but perhaps a little flighty. She believed men, you see, when they told her what she wanted to hear..."

I couldn't help but enjoy the irony.

"Wouldn't you have any ideas from where she was returning when you first saw her?" asked Holmes, like a dog reluctant to let go of a well-chewed slipper.

"Well, I don't approve of malicious gossip..." Mrs. Porter started.

"Of course not!" said Holmes. "Perish the thought! We're only trying to ascertain facts, here."

"You should keep your mouth shut, wife!" growled Porter.

Perhaps that, more than any of Holmes' entreaties, helped her make up her mind to talk.

"It seemed to me... Maybe... That she might have been returning from Scottwell Hill..."

"Scottwell Hill?" I asked.

"Lord Beltham's estate," the good woman replied.

Any observer less trained than I would have missed the minuscule flinch of the eye that I fleetingly saw across the face of my mentor when he heard that name.

"I think we have all we needed to know," said Holmes, rather abruptly. "Mrs. Porter, Mr. Porter, thank you both very much. We shall now be on our way."

What had Holmes discovered, I wondered, and how could it be connected with what I had found the previous night aboard the *Matilda Briggs*?

We stepped out of the Porters' farm and into the cab that had been waiting for us.

On the way back to Southampton, I finally had time to report in great details what I had learned the night before. I hadn't told him on the way to the Porters because I didn't wish to brag and was too curious about my mentor's apparent obsession with the farmers' testimony. But now I felt we had to put all the pieces of the puzzle on the table if we hoped to see a coherent picture emerge.

I concluded my account with:

"So, as you see, it is probably that the likely murderer is presently waiting for us in irons on the *Matilda Briggs*."

"You saw this Bill Sharper go ashore, wearing a gray suit?" asked Holmes.

"Yes. He left surreptitiously and I followed him all the way to that house, where I lost sight of him."

"And he hadn't resurfaced in the morning?"

"Not at 6 a.m., no. But he must have returned since and the delightful Captain Beech must have slapped him in irons."

"That is interesting, Harry, very interesting..."

I read his approval, perhaps even saw a note of pride, in his eyes, and felt greatly pleased at myself.

"You're a good assistant, Harry," he said. "I'm happy, yes, very happy to have you as my assistant... perhaps even my successor. I'm getting old, and this case will certainly be one of the last I will handle."

"Oh, Mr. Holmes..."

"If my suspicions are right, Harry, we have just un-covered the tip of a frightful iceberg. There'll be more blood spilled; more murders, of the same savage nature. We gave a horror beyond human comprehension—one that, I thought, had long been laid to rest. But now, I wonder... I wonder..."

I tried to get him to explain what he meant, but he vain. He seemed frozen in a state of deep concentration, ignoring everything around him.

But his prophetic words were soon revealed to be accurate!

As we crossed Lyndhurst on our way towards Southampton, we passed near the Commons, and stopped for a brief moment to take another look at the crime scene.

The police had removed the corpse; a simple wood-en barrier protected the spot where it had been found so that the onlookers and the morbidly curious would not trample it.

The bobby who stood near the barrier greeted us with respect, and remarked:

"People like that, Mr. Holmes, it would be better to wring their necks when they are born."

We nodded politely, but he continued:

"Another woman went missing, last night. Mrs. Murphy, a well-known piano teacher, beloved by everyone in Lyndhurst. She left home at 7 p.m. last night to go supervise a recital and hasn't been seen since. They found her hat, torn to pieces, on the Great Northern Road..."

Now, suddenly, our curiosity was inflamed.

"Where exactly?" asked Holmes.

The bobby pulled out his notebook, which contained a rough sketch of the area. I couldn't repress a gasp.

The place where the hat had been found was two miles north of the city. It was near the house where Bill Sharper had disappeared the night before—and just below the estate of Scottwell Hill!

Chapter VIII
Two Failures

Before checking in on the *Matilda Briggs*, we decided to have lunch at my hotel in Southampton.

"Perhaps we should investigate this new disappearance," I suggested. "Mrs. Murphy may be a new victim of our killer, although I'll be damned if I can figure how Bill Sharper might have done it..."

"Let's not rush to conclusions, Harry. This is still a simple disappearance that distraught minds may well have transformed into a bloody assault, but we have no evidence that an actual crime was committed."

I agreed with my mentor and nodded.

"Right now," he continued, "we only know what that bobby in Lyndhurst told us. She left home at 7 p.m. last night to supervise a recital and hasn't been seen since. Where was she going? The story about her hat, torn to pieces, is important. Was it really her hat? We are dealing with two possibilities: crime or accident. Which is it?"

"In fact," I observed, "I should begin by ascertaining Mrs. Murphy's age."

"Very good, Harry! Yes, you should find out if she was single, married or widowed. Leaving alone in the evening to attend a recital is unusual."

"Sharper might know where she is, or what happened to her," I hazarded.

"My dear Harry, criminals like this do not confess. I admit, everything seems to be against Sharper. Yet we have nothing tangible regarding the first murder, and only the location and the circumstances connect him to the piano teacher's disappearance."

"That's not quite true, Mr. Holmes. In the first case, Mrs. Porter reported seeing a huge man, dressed in a gray coat, exactly like Sharper's."

"You can't rely on what might be no more than a coincidence, my friend. But fear not, the evidence will come. You'll find out soon enough if Sharper is in irons aboard the *Matilda Briggs*, or has slipped through the net. But there are other cases waiting for me back in London, so I must leave this matter in your capable hands. Before I leave, however, I'd like to review what else needs to be investigated. First, Mrs. Murphy. Finding out what happened to her should be your first task. If it turns out she was killed by Sharper, you'll have the irrefutable proof of his guilt you've been seeking, won't you?"

I nodded again.

"I intend to search the house where I saw Sharper disappear. I might find more evidence of his crimes inside."

"*Alleged* crimes, Harry."

"Okay, alleged crimes, then."I sighed. "What about Scottwell Hill and Lord Beltham?" I asked. "They seem to be at the geographic intersection of Miss Beaton's murder and Mrs. Murphy's disappearance, not to mention being close to the white cottage. I remember reading about a Lord Beltham who was murdered in Paris ten years ago by his chauffeur, who turned out to be Fantômas..."

"Yes, that was Edward Beltham. The current holder of the title is William, his younger brother."

"Do you have any advice for me regarding how to handle him?"

"Only that you must move cautiously, or you might alert some very dangerous people, who could be in cahoots with our murderer."

"I note, Mr. Holmes, that you to longer seem to assume that the murder is the product of a fit of madness. If the killer has accomplices, it means that his attacks were planned... or, at the very least, that we are in the presence of a gang of like-minded criminals..."

"Not necessarily, Harry, the truth may yet be even stranger. As I told you a couple of days ago, *this is a story for which the world is not yet prepared*. But I have no doubt that it will yield to your sagacity, my young friend."

I bowed modestly and we drank our coffee in silence.

Then I accompanied my mentor back to the station and saw him to his train.

Once alone, I headed to the harbor.

It was necessary to ascertain if Bill Sharper had returned to the *Matilda Briggs*, even if it meant facing Captain Beech's foul mood.

Before I reached the place where the ship was moored, I hesitated. It displeased me to again have to call on the resources of the Police; on the other hand, the captain was sole master on board and totally free to deny me access.

As I approached, I noticed that the gangplank was raised, and an unusual commotion prevailed on the boat. The Captain, whom I saw coming and going, was shouting sharp orders and hurling formidable curses.

The timing to try to approach the old sea dog couldn't be worse.

I noticed a sailor leaning over the rail. Twice, I called to the man by making hand gestures, but obviously the word had been given that I was to be ignored, if I ever dared show my face again. He turned a deaf ear to my entreaties and finally walked away.

"All right," I said to myself. "The Harbor Master it is, then. I will find arguments to overcome Beech's obstinacy and his antipathy for detectives."

I did not hesitate and walked briskly to the office of Commissioner Jenkins, the Harbor Master. I introduced myself and showed him my papers. Then, I explained:

"Sir, it is urgent that you lend me your assistance in order to help in the capture of the prime suspect in the Lyndhurst murder case."

"Of course, sir," replied the Commissioner, a little old man with a twitchy left eye. "What do you need?"

"I must ascertain whether a certain crewman is still on board a ship or not."

"I don't understand," stammered Jenkins. "Is he part of her crew?"

"Yes, sir, but this sailor—a beastly creature if there was ever one!—was not there when I went looking for him at 6 a.m.. However, he might have returned since. It is to determine this that I need your help. The captain is also an underhanded brute who has forbidden me access to his ship."

"In this case, I will accompany you, sir. What is the name of that ship? And of her captain?"

"She is the *Matilda Briggs*, Commissioner, and her Captain is Arthur Beech."

"Ah..." His face took a forlorn expression. "But the *Matilda Briggs* was scheduled to set sail at 2 p.m. You just missed her, sir."

I rushed out of the Harbor Master like a crazy man and ran to the dock, screaming:

"Sharper! Sharper!"

The berth where the *Matilda Briggs* had been moored was now empty.

"You missed her by less than ten minutes," said a sailor wearing a tank top, pointing his outstretched arm towards the horizon.

There, among a tangle of masts of all kinds, I made out a small white dot that glided over the waters of Southampton Water, speeding out towards the sea.

It was the *Matilda Briggs*!

My first task had been a resounding failure. I could only hope that I would perform better in the investigation of the disappearance of Mrs. Murphy.

I hired a cab and instructed the driver to take me to Scottwell Hill.

I knew the road well. My legs still ached at the memory of that fateful night's journey made on foot.

As we drove past the white cottage, I couldn't repress a shudder. It seemed as empty and desolate as the night before.

Scottwell Hill, the estate of Lord Beltham was located less than mile away from the white cottage, just outside Lyndhurst's city limits. It consisted of a 5000-acre property with a beautifully designed park. In the center was Beltham Hall, a magnificent country house in the Jacobethan style.

I was greeted by a butler named Haxby, who went to inquire if the Lord of the House could see me despite my showing up uninvited, and returned quickly to tell me his master as waiting for me in the library.

Lord Beltham was in his mid-forties. He had a pleasant, open face with a square jaw, blue eyes, blond hair with a small beard, mustache and whiskers. He also wore a pair of spectacles.

He got up from behind his desk when Haxby ushered me in.

He cast a glance at my business card and examined me from head to toe over his spectacles. This quick review seemed to satisfy him, because he gave me his hand and, in a pleasant voice, said:

"Welcome to Beltham Hall, Mr. Dickson. I presume I owe the honor of your visit to the disappearance of Mrs. Murphy. How can I be of help to you?"

"I am assisting Mr. Sherlock Holmes in his investigation and am merely trying to gather facts about Mrs. Murphy and the circumstances of her disappearance," I replied. "I understand from the Police that she is a piano teacher and came here last night to supervise a recital?"

"That is correct. Every year, we put on a charity pantomime for the children of Lyndhurst, and Mrs. Murphy is kind enough to provide the musical accompaniment. Come, I'll show you..."

He took me to a magnificent ballroom with a grand piano and a small stage in a corner.

"This is where she played last night."

"I see. When did she arrive and when did leave?"

"She arrived around 7:30 p.m. The rehearsal began at 8 p.m., and was over by midnight. Haxby had set up a late night collation for the performers... I think she left just after midnight."

"On foot?"

"Naturally not!' replied Lord Bentham, shocked. "As I told the Police earlier, I had sent my chauffeur pick her up, and I had instructed him to wait and take her home when she was ready to go."

"I will need to talk to him."

"Of course. Haxby will arrange it."

"And he returned promptly?" I asked.

"I wasn't there when he did; I had already gone to bed, but I have no reason to assume he didn't. Charles has been in my employ for years."

"If your man, Charles, dropped Mrs. Murphy at home, how could her hat have ended up torn to pieces on the Great Northern Road? It was her hat, wasn't it?"

"Yes, or at least, that is what the police told me. It was identified by her neighbor. But to answer your question, I'm as confused as you are, Mr. Dickson. The whole thing seems darned impossible."

"I do not suspect your driver, My Lord," I said with less sincerity than I hoped to convey, "but it's hard to fathom what might have lured Mrs. Murphy out later that night... What kind of woman was she?"

"Well, she is middle-aged; never married, I believe. The daughter of a naval officer. She's been working at the local school for ten, fifteen years perhaps. Very serious; loves her music. I beg you to believe that I should not have hired her without being absolutely sure of her character. She taught the piano to my daughter Alice. She has a maid in her employ, who comes during the day. The police interrogated her and the poor girl has no idea what happened to her mistress."

I defended myself from being seen as trying to insinuate that there was something unwholesome about the perfectly honorable Mrs. Murphy.

"I didn't mean to cast aspersions on her character, My Lord," I protested. "Does she have relatives, friends perhaps, who might give us an idea about what might have happened to her?"

"She had many friends in the community. The parents of students, whom I'm sure will be happy to help your inquiry. I believe she has a brother, somewhere in

Yorkshire. But, I repeat, this line of inquiry seems absurd to me."

"Mr. Holmes is also looking into the death of Miss Betty Beaton..."

"Yes, the Lyndhurst Murder... I've heard about it. How awful!"

"You can see how tempting it is to connect the two incidents?"

"Yet I can't think of anything they have in common."

Indeed, I had to concede that Lord Beltham had a point.

I did not wish to abuse the kindness of this gentleman, whom I'm sure had other matters to attend, but I was only moderately satisfied with the result of my visit.

"Very well, My Lord. I only have one more question. Do you know who rents the small white cottage which is only half a mile down the road?"

Lord Beltham looked at me, surprised.

"The white cottage, you say?"

"Yes."

"How can this poor dwelling excite your curiosity?"

"It's hard to explain," I said. "I am surprised that it seems uninhabited, while its garden appears very well tended."

Lord Beltham smiled in his blond beard.

"Pardon me, sir," he said. "I know you are a detective, but I own the house to which you refer, and there's no mystery there. In fact, it is rented by two of my best employees."

"Really?"

"There is nothing surprising about that. The Estate owns a number of farms and cottages in the vicinity, which are rented to many people in its employ... For what reason are you so interested in this particular cottage?"

I was somewhat taken aback, and it bothered me to say too much about what had transpired the night before. On the other hand, I had to answer Lord Beltham's question, or risk being taken for a lunatic.

"I kept a watch over it last night, on the road, for reasons that I can't reveal as of yet..."

Lord Beltham looked at me with curiosity.

"The notion came to me to seek shelter in that cottage," I continued, "and I knocked several times, but no one answered..."

"What time was it?"

"Just after midnight."

"Then your timing was ill chosen," Lord Beltham said.

"Why?"

"Because the cottage was empty when you knocked. This is the home of two of my farmhands, the Johnson brothers, two single men who live alone. They are good workers. I intend to promote the elder one to foreman next month, as a matter of fact. But they were both working building the sets for the pantomime last night."

His Lordship's statement surprised me. If the tenants of the cottage were absent, who then had opened the door for Bill Sharper?

The fact that he had gone inside the cottage was undeniable. What happened to him thereafter remained a mystery.

I hadn't told Lord Beltham the truth and decided that it had been a mistake. My reluctance to share the whole story could only thicken the darkness that I sought to dispel. The best thing now was to open up to this gentleman.

"I have a confession to make, My Lord," I said, "and I can but hope that you will pardon me for not having told you the complete truth..."

Lord Beltham raised a quizzical eyebrow.

"I stood watch over the Johnson brothers' house last night, but it was because I was on the trail of a terrible criminal. I had followed him on foot from Southampton all the way to the house in question. It was he who knocked on the door, not I, and someone did let him in."

Lord Beltham looked pensive. He removed his spectacles and wiped them carefully with his handkerchief. Then he raised his head and looked at me with his myopic eyes.

"The man you were following, he was connected to the Lyndhurst Murder, was he not?"

"Yes. He is, in fact, our prime suspect."

"And it was just after midnight, you said?" he asked.

"Yes."

"And someone opened the door?"

"Yes."

"Are you sure of that?"

"Absolutely sure."

Lord Beltham replaced the spectacles on his nose.

"This is strange! Quite strange!" he whispered. "At midnight, the Johnson brothers were still both in the workshop. Is it possible that your man opened the door of the house himself, and just went in?"

"No. I definitely heard him knock, and someone unlocked the door from the inside."

"But you didn't see anyone let him in?"

I admitted that I had not.

"So that is not proof, Mr. Dickson. All my cottages are equipped with so-called safety locks which can be opened from outside with a key. It is possible that your bandit, if he had such a key, or even a fake in his possession, let himself in after no one answered his knocks."

Lord Beltham's theory left me pondering for a moment. Could Bill Sharper, a sailor just arrived in Southampton, be in possession of a false key and precise directions to a house which he knew would be unoccupied? It seemed unlikely.

"When your man came out," asked His Lordship, "did you notice anything else unusual?"

"There's the rub, My Lord. He did not come out—and therein lies the mystery."

"He did not come out, you say! Are you sure he didn't leave by the small back door?"

"I thought he might have, but I could not tell, because it was too late by the time I discovered the existence of a second exit."

"So you also have no incontrovertible evidence that he didn't manage to escape that way."

Lord Beltham had all the appearances of reason and I was forced to agree.

"What did you do then?" he asked.

"I stayed watching the house until 6 a.m. when the workers and the farmers started going about their business."

"So you must have seen the Johnson brothers return home?"

I paused. I certainly had not seen anything like it, and said so to His Lordship.

"It wouldn't have taken them much time... They must have left just after midnight, too..."

"At the same time as Mrs. Murphy."

"Why, yes, of course. But Mrs. Murphy has nothing to do with this. In fact, everyone left at about the same time. Ah! This is all very strange indeed... Perhaps it would be best if I were to question them?"

"Please, Your Lordship, do nothing for the time being!" I entreated. "There's still too much darkness about this case, and the slightest indiscretion might cripple our investigation."

"As you wish, sir," condescended Lord Beltham. "As far as I'm concerned, the Johnson brothers, whom I consider to be honest people, are victims and not accomplices, as you seem to assume..."

There were more mysteries here that my brain could handle. This case was becoming a Chinese puzzle, and I needed to be alone to work it out at my leisure. Furthermore, I didn't want to take further advantage of Lord Beltham's kindness.

However, moved by a sudden stroke of inspiration, I said:

"One last question, My Lord: Have you ever heard of the *Matilda Briggs*?"

It was as if the proverbial thunderbolt had struck His Lordship. He became so pale and so unsteady on his feet that, for a moment, I was afraid he might faint right in front of me.

I extended my arm to give him support, but he pushed it back, rather harshly.

"No, never," he said curtly. "Now you must excuse me, Mr. Dickson, I have spent as much time with you as I could afford; I have urgent business which needs to be dealt with."

He rang; Haxby returned and escorted me back to the front door, where my taxi was waiting.

I climbed into it and instructed the driver to return to my hotel in Southampton.

I found myself more confused than before. I still believed Bill Sharper was our man, but there was obviously far more to this crime than met the eye. I felt that I had failed to get the truth out of Lord Bentham, just as I had failed to arrest Sharper before the *Matilda Briggs* set sail.

Our goal seemed more elusive than before. How could I, following my mentor's methods, find the truth in this maze of deception?

Back at the Star Hotel, I slouched in an armchair, lit a pipe and started thinking.

I had incurred several failures. Was my star waning and a perfidious destiny suddenly working against me?

Had I let the new Jack the Ripper escape justice?

I wondered if Captain Beech might be an accomplice in the plot, then summarily rejected this idea as preposterous. It was only my anger at having been outsmarted that made me see accomplices and suspects everywhere.

I resolved to try harder to fight off the injustice of fate.

What to do next?

I remained convinced that Sharper was the Lyndhurst murderer, but was he also the killer of Mrs. Murphy? In any event, now he was very likely sailing away, free as a bird, on the *Matilda Briggs*, a ship that carried a secret obviously shared by my master and Lord Beltham, but still a mystery to me.

Were the Johnson brothers, the residents of the white cottage, also accomplices? Were they innocent victims or bold malefactors? And if not them, according to Lord Beltham's testimony, who had opened the door to let Bill Sharper inside?

And what had been Sharper's goal in visiting that cottage? Who as he meeting there? For what purpose? Sharper, the man with countless crimes, endowed with superhuman strength, the prey to nameless passions, could not turn into a simple, ordinary burglar!

That was crazy... ridiculous!

And what about Mrs. Murphy's disappearance? Unlike the Lyndhurst crime, her murder was still only a hypothesis, gossip from the scandal-hungry newspapers.

Having laid out all the facts known to me in my mind, I recovered some of my assurance and decided that the first thing to do was to try to apprehend Bill Sharper.

The *Matilda Briggs* had left Southampton, true, but there was such a thing as international justice. At any port in the world where she moored, I could request the local police to board her and arrest the bandit.

I went out again, ignoring the bell that summoned the guests of the Hotel for dinner.

The cool evening air and the sea breeze completed the restoration of my good spirits.

I returned to the Harbor Master office where the little old man with whom I had dealt earlier received me despite the fact he was about to leave for the day and hand his duties to the night commissioner.

"Well? What do you want now?" he asked when he saw me.

"A small favor," I replied. "Could you tell me the *Matilda Briggs*' next port of call?"

The Harbor Master consulted a large register with a black cover, and answered:

"Hamburg... Yes, that is the next stop on Captain Beech's log... but, you know, those pesky sailboats can always find a good excuse to divert to another destination... Headwinds, or God knows what else..."

"Let's suppose that she actually goes to Hamburg... How long will it take for her to reach that port?"

"Four to five days... maybe six."

"Excellent! I have time to notify the Hamburg police!"

I thanked the brave officer profusely then ran out. My first concern was to send a cablegram to the Hamburg police.

I stopped at the police station and, after presenting my credentials and explaining the situation to the Sergeant in charge, I was allowed to send a telegram requesting the temporary arrest of Bill Sharper.

Afterward, I returned to my hotel and decided to skip dinner and go to bed as I had a terrible headache.

The moment I entered the lobby, a porter, who seemed to be expecting me, handed me a message. I opened it immediately.

This note came from Lord Beltham and contained the following message:

New information. Come tomorrow 9 a.m.

Pulling a pen from my pocket, I asked the porter to send two messages. The first was a reply to Lord Beltham confirming I would indeed be there; the second to Sherlock Holmes asking him to come and meet me at the Hotel at noon.

CHAPTER IX
The Shadow of the Past

Thursday, June 9th

The next morning, I woke up hungry.

After enjoying a hearty English breakfast, I took a cab back to Scottwell Hill.

During the journey, I let the side window open and the cool morning air helped put my ideas into place.

When I arrived at Beltham Hall, Haxby quickly answered the bell and took me to his master who was, like the day before, in the library.

Lord Beltham seemed impatient to see me.

"Please, excuse me for my conduct of yesterday, Mr. Dickson," he said, holding out his hand. "I was wrong to have dismissed you so curtly."

I made a polite gesture of absolution, and waited for him to continue.

"I called you in here this morning because I have some new information..."

"New information about Mrs. Murphy's disappearance?"

"Sadly, no."

"So, what is it?"

"As I told you, the Johnson brothers worked all night here the day before yesterday until about 5 or 5:30 a.m. I was able to ascertain that by talking to my foreman..."

"This confirms that they're not the ones who opened to door of the white cottage. We already suspected this, My Lord."

"Yes, but what I didn't know was that they had someone staying at that house that night. So it was not empty after all!"

"Ah-ha! And do we know who that someone might be?"

"Alas, no. I learned of this from my foreman, whom I questioned last night, after your departure. He said he wanted to send the brothers home around 2 a.m., but they said they'd rather stay here and finish the work, *and not disturb the friend who was staying with them!*"

"Good Heavens! That is important!" I snapped my fingers like a kid who's just won a game of marbles. "So this is the man who opened the door to Sharper..."

"Sharper?"

"The man I was following... The prime suspect in the Lyndhurst murder."

"Ah yes! The man who's vanished."

"Precisely."

Then, I added somewhat ruefully:

"Although I have some evidence that he may be presently en route to Hamburg on a shop called the *Matilda Briggs*."

Lord Beltham looked at me, stunned. A cloud passed over his face, which suddenly bore a grief-stricken look.

"Oh, no," he whispered.

"Perhaps if Your Lordship were to tell me the full story—in strictest confidence, of course—it might cast a light on this murky affair?"

"I don't really see how it could, but it seems I must trust you, Mr. Dickson. Besides, I believe that your mentor already knows all I'm going to tell you—and possibly a good deal more..."

Ah-ah! I thought! *The truth at last!*

"The *Matilda Briggs* will always be linked to our family's greatest shame," began Lord Beltham. "It belonged to my older brother, Edward..."

"The one who was murdered by his aide-de-camp Gurn in Paris ten years ago? Gurn, who turned out be the notorious criminal Fantômas."

"The truth is a little more complex. The man the world knew as Gurn grew up here, at Scottwell Hill, with my brother and me."

I could not help but betray my utter amazement at this unheard-of revelation.

"We knew him as 'Alan.' He was an orphan, found by Reverend Patterson of Lyndhurst, who entrusted him to our family at age 7. Unfortunately, Alan fell under my brother's evil influence, for as much as it pains me, I must confess, Mr. Dickson, that Edward as close to being evil incarnate as any villain who ever walked the Earth..."

"Lord Beltham... A villain...?"

"A murderer whose litany of crimes is still only very incompletely known today. For instance, it was he who, while living in disgrace in Berlin in 1893, coined the fear-inspiring alias of 'Fantômas' to commit a series of murders—all with the help of Alan who operated at the time under the alias of 'Juan North.'"

"I can barely believe what you're telling me, My Lord." I said with total honesty. "What happened next?"

"It's long story, but suffice it to say that Alan, now known as 'Gurn,' met my brother again during the Boer war in South Africa. More importantly, he met my sister-in-law Maud, whom Edward had married, hoping to use her own family connections on the Greystoke side to be allowed to return to England. I gather that their affair began on the ship bringing them back to England. A few months later, Edward surprised them in bed in his apartment in Paris. Alan strangled him and assumed the mantle of Fantômas."

"That is... fascinating. Who knows of this?"

"Your mentor, most assuredly. A few others, I suppose. But the matter was, for the most part, kept secret, not to embarrass the Royal family."

"I see... You mentioned that your brother had been forced to leave England in disgrace. I presume that had to do with the *Matilda Briggs*?"

"You are very astute, Mr. Dickson," replied Lord Beltham, with a thin, mirthless smile. "Around 1885, my brother took an interest in, and began to finance, the experiments of a madman named Moreau. The *Mathilda Briggs* belonged to our family and was used to supply Moreau on that island of his..."

"I believe I read a book about this," I interrupted, "but it didn't mention your family."

"Indeed! Mr. Wells somehow located a report made by a survivor named Pendrick, picked up by British Navy. But it had been heavily censored, again to preclude any likelihood of embarrassing the Royal Family."

"So it wasn't a fiction? Moreau really found a way to produce men-animal hybrids?"

"I know it to be so," replied Lord Beltham, "although I believe Mr. Wells embellished the truth somewhat to make room to express his socialist views. What mattered was that some of his most successful experiments were brought back to London aboard the *Matilda Briggs* to, er, take part in... hum... some special *soirées* organized by my brother to satisfy his and a few of his debauched friends' most perverted lust..."

Lord Beltham turned his head in shame, so painful was the memory. I said nothing, waiting for him to continue.

"The main attraction of these, er, *soirées* was a man ape, from a tribe of preternaturally advanced simians discovered on an Indonesian island during the Ache Rebellion in the 1870s.[7] Moreau had captured a couple of them and managed to evolve them even further. In the summer of 1888, that creature, whose name was Bom-Ko, managed to escape, several times, and killed several prostitutes, in the bloodiest manner..."

"You don't mean that..." I gasped, "Jack the Ripper..."

"Yes," he said, nodding. "The murderous maniac that the Press dubbed Jack the Ripper was none other than Bom-Ko. Understand that the poor thing was not doing this out of savagery or blood-lust; he had somehow convinced himself that, in order to become a true man, he had to absorb the life-force, and even eat the organs, of real men—or women, in this case..."

"What happened next?" I asked breathlessly.

"Your mentor, who had learned of Pendrick's account about Moreau's island through his brother Mycroft, quickly connected the dots and solved the mystery. However, as not only my brother but several other members of the aristocracy close to the Royal Family, were involved, the matter was kept tightly under wraps. Edward was forced to leave England; the scandal was sup-

---

[7] Readers wishing to find more about this tribe can read Jules Lermina's account *To-Ho and the Gold Destroyers*, Black Coat Press, ISBN 935558-34-7.

pressed; the *Matilda Briggs* and her crew were allowed to go free; and Moreau's island was shelled into oblivion by a British Destroyer on Mycroft Holmes's orders..."

"And Bom-Ko?"

"I believe he was euthanized."

A long silence ensued.

"You can now understand my horror at seeing that accursed name—the *Matilda Briggs*—return to haunt my family, again linked to a bloody murder and, through the white cottage, even more directly to me... I could have sworn that the Johnson brothers were good, honest people. Now I don't know what think..."

"It's too early to speculate about the guilt of your workers, My Lord," I said. "As for Bill Sharper, I don't even know for certain that he is aboard the *Matilda Briggs*, which set sail yesterday for Hamburg. I've cabled the local police to detain him, if he is on board."

"This is very strange and quite incomprehensible... and all this, plus the disappearance of Mrs. Murphy!"

Lord Beltham looked genuinely concerned.

"I gather you now feel less reassured about her fate?"

"What do you want me to tell you? There are so many extraordinary things here... I do not know what to think... She is my daughter's piano teacher..."

At that moment, a young, beautiful blonde girl, around 20, stepped into the room.

"Papa, did I hear you mention Mrs. Murphy? Has she been found?"

"Not yet, Alice. Come and meet Mr. Harry Dickson—one of the detectives looking for her."

I shook hands with the young woman.

"Alice is engaged to Dr. Smythe, the director of Manor House, the Minstead Asylum," explained Lord

Beltham. "We were planning to announce their betrothal after the fête. I'm a financial benefactor of the place and we're opening a new wing next week."

"My mentor and I are working hard to solve this case," I began.

"Your mentor... The famous Sherlock Holmes?" she said, her eyes growing bigger.

"Yes, indeed. I've asked him to come down and am scheduled to meet him at my hotel at noon."

"I tell you what," interrupted Lord Beltham. "Let me send a car for him and we'll have lunch here. I would like him to oversee the interrogation of my Chauffeur, Charles, and of the Johnson brothers and even the search of the white cottage—if you don't mind, Mr. Dickson?"

"Naturally, not," I said. "How could I? My mentor will be thrilled, I'm sure."

"That's settled then," said Lord Beltham, clapping his hands.

Haxby arrived and His lordship gave him a series of brief instructions. Then he returned to me, and offered me what looked like an excellent Havana.

I took the cigar, lit it and, after a moment, asked:

"My Lord... If you don't mind... I didn't have time to look at the local papers when I left the hotel this morning. Is there anything new reported about Mrs. Murphy's case?"

"See for yourself," said Lord Beltham, handing me a copy of *The Daily Mail*.

I cast a quick glance on the tidbits devoted to the disappearance of Mrs. Murphy. Nothing caught my eye that was worth the trouble of further investigation. They again mentioned the hat found on the road, the orderly habits of the victim and the crime of Lyndhurst. To my delight, no one even alluded to having seen a man in a gray suit.

"Nothing, am I right?" Lord Beltham asked.

"Less than nothing. The journalists have left us a clear field, so we can act with discretion. It's the only service they can render us, really."

"Until noon, what do you plan to do?"

"I won't try anything until the arrival of Sherlock Holmes... One question, though: Will we find the Johnson brothers at home when we search their house?"

"Yes. I told my foreman to send them home."

"Excellent. And do we have your permission to ask your driver any questions we'd like?"

"Yes, indeed. As much as you like. Mrs. Murphy's disappearance—possibly, murder—has been of great concern to Charles. Frankly, I think he's about to lose his head completely".

"That's quite normal," I replied. He was, after all, the last man to have seen this lady. I'd be surprised if he wasn't worried."

I let His Lordship return to his correspondence and took a walk through the gardens. From a small belvedere located on an elevated part of the estate, I could see the little white cottage which, in my mind, I now thought of as the "scene of the crime," even though I was still unsure as to what crime might have been committed there.

The shutters were open, the windows also opened wide. In the sun, the house looked completely innocent, as if it had nothing of which to be ashamed.

I saw no one around, which meant nothing, since the Johnson brothers were probably still sleeping. The laundry was drying in the garden and, without Lord Beltham's statements, I would have believed in the presence of a housewife in this mysterious "home."

I waited in the garden until a clock told me it was half past eleven. Holmes would have arrived in Southampton, where Lord Beltham had sent a car to pick him up.

I resolutely turned away from my contemplation of the countryside and returned to the manor.

Half an hour later, I heard the noise of a car pulling up the driveway and stopping in front of Beltham Hall.

Sherlock Holmes had arrived.

CHAPTER X
Sherlock Holmes Investigates

The great detective's arrival gave me a welcome respite and provided me with the opportunity to further study my mentor's methods. A wise man can always draw some useful information from the work of a master.

Holmes gave no indication that he and Lord Beltham had previously met. Of course, he didn't yet know that His lordship had told me about his family's nefarious connections to the *Matilda Briggs* and the Jack the Ripper murders.

We were soon talking about the crime of Lyndhurst and the disappearance of Mrs. Murphy over an excellent luncheon that had been served in the dining room.

I reported my actions of the day before, and my failure in securing the presence of Bill Sharper before the *Matilda Briggs* sailed for Hamburg.

Holmes, however, did not appear distraught at the news, and congratulated me for having sent a telegram to the Germans.

Lord Beltham inquired if my mentor had arrived at any conclusions, but Holmes waved the question aside with an evasive gesture:

"Don't ask me anything yet, My Lord," he said. "Before I can answer, I must hear the witnesses."

So Lord Beltham asked Haxby to fetch Charles, the driver.

He was a big man, verging on fifty; he entered the room, somewhat out of breath and red as a poppy flower.

His Lordship invited him to take a seat and he sat there, staring at us, one after the other, with frightened eyes.

"Charles," His lordship said, "these two gentlemen are going to ask you some questions. I want you to answer them, frankly and fully, and try not to omit anything."

The driver looked at his master with a bewildered air.

"Charles," Holmes began, "it was you who took Mrs. Murphy home on the night of Tuesday to Wednesday?"

"Yes, sir."

"You know this lady very well?"

"Oh, certainly... I see her here often. I'm the one who drives her back after Miss Alice's lessons."

"At what time did Mrs. Murphy leave in your car?"

The chauffeur hesitated, then said:

"That, sir, I cannot tell you exactly... Maybe one a.m., maybe half past one..."

"Not earlier?"

"No. The rehearsals had just finished."

"I can confirm this," interrupted Lord Beltham. "Mrs. Murphy left with the last guests."

"Perfect!" Holmes said. "And you drove her directly to her home in Southampton?"

"Er... That is to say..." answered Charles.

"You don't seem to be sure. Why? Didn't you drive directly to Southampton?"

"Well, er, yes, I did, sir. I left her right outside her home on Chapel Lane, just as His Lordship had asked me to do."

"Very well. Did you check to see if Mrs. Murphy actually went inside?"

Charles remained silent. Holmes stared at the driver:

"You seem to hesitate again, my friend. Nobody here is accusing you... Speak frankly. Did you see her go inside?"

"Er... I guess she must have done..."

"Did you notice if Mrs. Murphy was still wearing her hat?"

"She had to wear it, didn't she?"

"Couldn't you tell?"

"Well, it was dark..."

"Did you return straight to Scottwell Hill afterward?"

"Yes, sir."

"What time was it when you arrived?"

"Around two... two-thirty...:"

Holmes sighed and leaned back in his chair.

"I find your testimony rather vague. Remember that this is a very serious case. Possibly even murder... Let us review what you've told us..."

Charles made an angry movement:

"I told you everything I know," he said. "I can't tell you anymore. You're not accusing me of murder, are you?"

Now Holmes got up and stood in front of the man:

"No, I do not accuse you of anything, but what I ask of you is to tell me the truth."

"Well, yes, I know, but you all seem to suspect me of foul play... I can see that..."

"You must admit, Charles, that your answers are, at the very least, misleading. Beware, do not try to deceive us any further!"

Under fire from Holmes, the driver became disturbed. Suddenly, the words choked in his throat. He burst into heavy sobs and we thought he was going to faint.

"Speak the truth now," ordered Holmes, almost as if he was commanding a subject under hypnosis.

"I'll be honest. Yes, I will tell you the truth, sirs," stammered the chauffeur. "His lordship will no doubt fire me, but never mind! I don't want anyone to suspect me anymore!"

We all leaned forward, prey to an unquenchable curiosity. Would Charles finally give us the key to this maddening riddle?

The big man whispered:

"I made a mistake, I admit it... A serious mistake... but I swear, I didn't kill Mrs. Murphy!"

"Explain yourself," Holmes insisted.

"Er... I did not think we would need the car that late at night... I have a nephew, a good buy named Justin, who has a girlfriend... A sweet little Irish girl named Harriet. He wanted to impress her, so I loaned him the car... Since his mother—my sister—passed away, I can't deny the lad anything, and sometimes, he takes advantage of my weakness. He wanted to drive young Harriett home after the party, so he asked me to lend him the car. I was wrong to do it, but as I told you, I'm just too fond of that damned nephew! So he took the car and left, promising me to be back in under an hour... It was just after midnight. I don't know what he did then, but when His Lordship asked me to take Mrs. Murphy home, that rascal of a nephew of mine hadn't yet returned. So lost my head and I stupidly hid in the garage behind a barrel of petrol. Mrs. Murphy called me two or three times, then I heard someone offering to take her home. She went with another guest... But who? I don't know."

"Why did you not reveal this earlier?" Holmes asked.

"Because I was at fault, sir, and my nephew, too. It took this murder accusation to untie my tongue. You see, I did not drive Mrs. Murphy home... And if that poor lady got murdered, maybe it's my fault, but I'm not the one who did it! No, never!"

Charles' story plunged us into the greatest astonishment. Now we were certain that Charles had not murdered the piano teacher.

Holmes kept up the stern look that had ripped the confession from the big man's throat.

"There are still a number of points that remain to be clarified, such as the presence of the hat on road. For us to fully believe your story," he said, "you'll have to bring your nephew to talk to us."

"That is, if you want to keep your job," added Lord Beltham.

"Oh, thank you, Your Lordship! He lives in the city, sir," Charles replied, meaning Southampton. "He comes home only at night, but I doubt I'm going to see him soon, especially after what he did to me that night."

"Then, you will have to fetch him," said Holmes.

"Right now?"

"Certainly."

Charles consulted Lord Beltham who, with a gesture, dismissed the driver.

"Do as Mr. Holmes said."

The unfortunate driver sheepishly left, making gestures of gratitude to us.

"Don't you think, Mr. Holmes," I said after Charles had left, "that it might have been better to keep this man at our disposal?"

"No, he's merely a simple, ordinary man who made a mistake, nothing more. He is not guilty of anything serious that might concern the Law."

"So what do you think happened to Mrs. Murphy?" asked Lord Beltham.

Holmes sat down and began to fill his pipe conscientiously.

"We now know she left with some person as yet unknown. Was she assaulted on the road as the presence of her hat found in the state that you know would indicate? I'm not so certain. The lady has not returned home, but the mystery of her disappearance will be solved when we find how that hat came to be there... In the meanwhile, there remains the matter of the house where you, Harry, saw a man who was, and still is, our prime suspect, disappear. This is where we must carry on our investigation. We must search that house thoroughly, after ascertaining the whereabouts of the two Johnson brothers."

Lord Beltham looked at his watch. It was now a little after 3 p.m.

"They must be working in their garden; they won't disturb us."

We were eager to begin and the progress that Holmes had made in the investigation of the disappearance of Mrs. Murphy had obvious greatly impressed Lord Beltham, who made no objections.

"We shall need them to be in attendance, My Lord," said Holmes, "but would you have any problem if I were to summon two policemen to assist us in this most delicate stage in our inquiry?"

"Not at all, Mr. Holmes. Say the word, and Haxby will call for them right away."

"Excellent. Of course, you will accompany us, sir," Holmes added. "You are, after all, the owner of the property in question and must have access at any time."

"I am at your service,' His Lordship said, conquered by the masterful detective.

"Perfect! Then, come along, gentlemen! It is time we took a look at that house!"

CHAPTER XI
The Mysterious Letters

The white cottage was, as I said, less than half a mile from Scottwell Hill.

We waited to leave until the two policemen, whose presence Haxby had requested, had arrived.

Then we left together on foot and it took us barely ten minutes before we arrived at the mysterious house.

Lord Beltham knocked on the door.

The same noise of locks that was burned into my memory was heard immediately. The door opened and a man in a blue flannel shirt, gray-haired, looking barely awake, stood before us.

"My Lord?" he asked, acknowledging his boss's presence with a nod of his head.

"Yes, Dick," said Lord Beltham, in a grim tone of voice. "Is your brother with you?"

"He's asleep, My Lord," replied Dick Johnson. "His job is hard, as you know. It was very kind of you to give us the day off, especially after we worked nights most of this week."

While speaking, Dick, the eldest of the two brothers, glanced stealthily and worriedly at Sherlock Holmes and me.

I immediately sensed that his conscience was not clear.

We stepped inside. A wide staircase stood in the middle of the hallway.

Dick Johnson took the lead, and we followed him in silence. Arriving at a small door, he knocked with his fist, shouting:

"Jim! Jim! Wake up! His Lordship is here!"

Then he opened and we found ourselves in a room with two beds, whitewashed walls, a simple table, two chairs and a wardrobe.

The brother, who had indeed been sleeping, got up and staggered towards us, saluting us in a slurred voice.

He was younger, although his wrinkles and wilting skin, blackened by the indelible traces of hard labor, made him look older than his true age.

The two workers looked at us without understanding, or rather perhaps fearing to accurately guess the motive that had brought us to their home.

"Let us sit down," said Lord Beltham, sitting on the edge of one of the beds, to let us take the chairs.

But Holmes simply remained standing, his hands pressed behind his back, and asked the brothers point blank:

"So you were asleep?"

"Yes, sir," stammered the elder of the two brothers. "His lordship will tell you... We worked nights most of this week."

Lord Beltham nodded.

"Did you work the night of Tuesday to Wednesday?"

"Yes, sir," said the elder of the two brothers. "His Lordship knows we worked hard on building the sets for the fête. We even finished work some others who'd left early hadn't completed."

"That's right," said Jim.

"So this house was empty on Tuesday night?"

The two brothers exchanged a quick glance.

"Answer my question," Holmes insisted. "Yes or no, was this house empty that night?"

"Er, yes, it was," said Dick.

"But didn't you tell your foreman that you had a friend staying with you, that night."

Dick Johnson hesitated a few seconds, then said:

"Ah yes! Now I recall, sir! It was an old friend, from our last job... He didn't feel very well that night, so we told him he could spend the night here."

"That's strange, because my friend here," said Holmes, pointing at me, "remembers the door being opened just past midnight to admit a stranger."

This time, the two brothers said nothing.

The silence continued, sinister, like the darkness after a bolt of lightning.

I noticed that Dick, the older brother, slowly moved back towards the wall, as if he felt in need of support. Jim, on the contrary, seemed more in control of himself. He looked at Holmes and said in a firm voice:

"Could it be, sir, that you're accusing us of something?"

"I accuse no one," answered the great detective, "but someone else might..."

"Who?" stammered the younger of the two brothers.

We all admired the quiet and masterful way with which Holmes was slowly pulling the Johnson brothers into his net.

Both looked at him with fixed pupils, extraordinarily dilated in their dark orbits; it was singularly impressive.

Suddenly Holmes clapped his hands together, which made us all jump, so much tension there was in the air.

"Bill Sharper might. Who opened the door to let him in?"

The name fell like the blow of an axe.

Jim turned pale and looked at his brother.

Holmes repeated:

"Who opened the door to let Sharper in?"

Lord Beltham's mouth hung slightly open. The two policemen were frozen like statues.

My mentor left his station and slowly walked to the elder of the two brothers. Then, staring into his eyes, he said only:

"Sharper talked..."

Dick turned away, his gray-haired head swinging slowly in a gesture of negation.

"I don't know what you mean," he replied feebly.

Jim, on the other hand, had not lost his composure, which, confronted with Holmes' assurance, seemed extraordinary to me.

"Show them," my mentor said coldly, motioning to the policemen.

One of the bobbies took a package, hastily wrapped in a newspaper from under his jacket.

Sparing no drama, Holmes unfolded the wrapping.

Some dusty tassels appeared, then blue taffeta roses, leafless and horribly flat. It was Mrs. Murphy's hat, that had been found on the road to Southampton, not far from here.

"Do you recognize this?" Holmes asked.

This time, I noticed that the two brothers' faces relaxed and they seemed to breathe easier, as if my mentor had just made a mistake.

"No," they said at once.

"It's a woman's hat," Jim added, unmoved.

"And this woman's body may well be here," said Holmes.

He walked to the door and, on the threshold, gestured to the two policemen, instructing them to drag the brothers after us.

The Johnson brothers, with heavy steps, followed us downstairs on the creaking steps.

"To the garden!" Holmes commanded.

In a single file, we passed through the little door that I had noticed the night I had been watching the house.

I recognized the garden, with its vegetable beds, all carefully maintained, and its narrow paths, well raked.

I immediately realized that Holmes suspected that the Johnson brothers' mysterious guest had buried Mrs. Murphy's corpse, with Bill Sharper's help.

But, unless they had replanted rows of carrots and cabbages over the grave, it didn't strike me as believable that this garden could have been used to bury a body.

The calm assurance of the two brothers was an indication that, this time, Holmes might be following the wrong lead.

However, he ignored the rows of vegetables and stopped in front of a pile of manure stick in a corner, against the walls, which I had ignored.

His foot probed the ground, then stopped for a moment.

"Perhaps we'll find something here," he said.

"Unlikely," I said. "I would certainly have noticed the signs while I was keeping watch."

"They might have buried the body later, after you'd left."

"True," I said, "but engaging in this macabre task in broad daylight would have been damn careless."

"All right,' said Holmes. "We can always return, if necessary, with men equipped with shovels. Let's return inside."

Again, in single file, we went back into the house.

The two policemen thoroughly searched a storage space on the ground floor. We opened crates, moved empty barrels and even disturbed a pile of logs stacked in a corner.

"There is body in this house somewhere," affirmed Holmes, stamping on the ground with an air of total certainty. "It can't be otherwise."

The two brothers were avoiding our eyes again. It was impossible to guess what was going on in those dark souls.

The kitchen, small and spotlessly clean, was searched, then we headed back to the first floor.

Nothing escaped my mentor's eye.

In the hallway, there was a long trunk of somber aspect which I had noticed earlier. This chest was covered with old leather, jagged iron and sealed with a double steel lock. Obviously, it had also caught my mentor's attention. He walked right over.

"Open it," enjoined Holmes, pointing to the huge object.

I then observed the figure of the older brother sagging; I thought it was as good as a confession. This was one of those typical triggers common among criminals, who always fight against the inevitable finding and exposure of the secrets that will confirm their guilt.

"Open it!" repeated the great detective.

The miserable creature hesitated; his hands wandered as if they were grasping some invisible support to appease his distress.

Jim came to the aid of his older brother.

"The keys are in the dining room," he said.

"Go get them," ordered Holmes.

We followed Jim Johnson back to the kitchen; he grabbed a bunch of keys of various types that were hanging over the fireplace.

At Holmes' urging, he bent down over the trunk, fiddled for a moment with the lock, until the heavy lid suddenly snapped opened, falling back against the wall.

Immediately a penetrating smell grabbed us by the throat, a smell both sour and sickly sweet, the kind of cadaverous stench that, as I imagine it, is exhaled by millennia-old tombs where mummies sleep wrapped in their bandages.

The inside of the trunk was carefully arranged and packed with clothes. There were twigs of dried lemon leaves and lavender between their folds, which explained the smell that had struck us when it had been opened.

Holmes bent over and, with a sudden gesture, overturned all the clothes.

Nothing!

"Remove the false bottom," he told Jim Johnson.

I cursed myself for missing this. Jim obeyed and removed the frame that separated the two parts of the huge chest.

We approached closer still.

All the bottom of the trunk were a few dusty old books bound in black leather. The presence of these humble volumes, which appeared to be of no value, suggested family heirlooms. I would have liked to see the titles, but my curiosity was presently directed at something else.

There were not only books in that chest. An oblong box, covered with a serge jacket, occupied the length of the secret compartment from one end to the other of the trunk.

"What is that?" Holmes asked.

That second box, slim and narrower, showed its age; it was a small case, brown and tarnished, covered with labels of various shipping companies.

Had we finally found the object of our search?

The brothers did not answer, and nothing but the convulsive trembling of Dick's shoulders betrayed the disarray of that soul. Jim, however, was still manifesting a surprising composure.

"Family papers," he answered in a low voice.

Inside, they were papers, indeed, and our disappointment was great when we noticed their confused mass. This chest contained no bloodied clues—only papers, in bundles and in stacks tied together by strings.

But Holmes was not disappointed.

He hastily looked at the documents contained in the trunk. They were, as Jim had stated, family papers, diplomas, certificates... the lifetime history of a poor family, meticulously collated and organized.

Suddenly, my mentor handed me a large document that he had just examined.

"So you were convicts?" he asked, turning to the Johnson brothers.

Jim bowed his head. All his previous assurance had now deserted him. As for Dick, he has weeping silently.

A sincere pity crept into my heart at the sight of this distress and I noticed that Lord Beltham was not unmoved either.

Holes continued impassively:

"You've done hard labor, but this is the certificate of good conduct, of the type issued to convicts upon their release. That will speak in your favor. Come, be frank. Your only hope now is your sincerity, the clemency of the judge... Come, speak! Where have you hidden Mrs. Murphy's body?"

To this direct question, Jim looked up and said:

"We didn't kill that lady! I assure you, sir!"

"Of course not. Sharper did it. But you helped him hide the body, didn't you?"

"No, we didn't!" clearly articulated Jim.

"Ah! ah! But you know who Bill Sharper is!"

Jim did not answer. Dick seemed totally lost to what was happening around him.

"You are wrong to deny it," said Holmes. "All the evidence is against you. Bill Sharper is known to you ... He came here to meet your mysterious friend... your partner in crime, most likely... Your denials are useless. Even if you're innocent of the murder, you will share responsibility for the other crime if you don't speak."

While Holmes was talking, I kept rifling through the papers. Suddenly a string broke and a packet of letters scattered on the ground.

I picked up a couple, looked at them, then showed them to Holmes.

"Look at this!" I said.

The two letters were written on poor quality paper and appeared to be by the same hand. Only the variations in the yellow tint of the paper showed that some were older than others.

The handwriting was almost indecipherable—crude beyond belief. But one thing jumped at me immediately: a sign identical at the end of each letter, an "S" clearly formed and intended to be a signature.

"What are these?" asked my mentor, suddenly putting one of the letters in front of Jim. "What does it mean? That "S', is it a signature fir Bill Sharper?"

The two brothers persisted in their silence.

Holmes took five or six similar letters. He compared the characters, checked the stamped envelopes, then, nodding slowly, said:

"What a find, Harry!" Notice that this letter is from early June 1906, postmarked from London. This one is from a year later, Portsmouth, and that one is from December 1908, Glasgow. You know what this means, don't you?"

"My word! That's when the *Matilda Briggs* stopped at each port!"

He agreed with a nod, then continued, waving a last envelope:

And finally, my dear friend, we find one last letter, from Southampton, dated Friday, June 3. This letter is still fresh. It dates from the arrival of the *Matilda Briggs* in the port of Southampton a week ago. At each stop of that dreadful three-master, a mysterious hand wrote the letters and sent them to this address. This hand is the same, and invariable signing 'S'—for Bill Sharper!"

The certainty with which my mentor built his case and the mechanical precision with which it gradually closed the defendants within a circle of deductions filled me with silent admiration.

Holmes took the letters and placed them under the eyes of the younger of the two brothers.

"Will you deny it again?" he asked in a shrill voice. "Admit it! You have never ceased to be in relation with Bill Sharper. On each of his stops, he wrote to you to let you know of his presence on British soil. You are his accomplices, his purveyors, perhaps?"

Jim sighed. One felt that he was exhausted and it was in a choked voice that he uttered:

"No, sir, no... It wasn't us that he wrote to..."

"But you acknowledge that it was he who sent those letters here?"

Livid, Jim nodded, but responded:

"Yes, but not to us..."

"Not to you? Then to whom?"

I took a second look at one of the letters and noticed that, in the top left corner was a single letter: "F."

"They were addressed to 'F,'" I said. "But who is 'F'?"

Holmes looked as perplexed as I was. And the two brothers were quivering in fear. It was obvious that they were too frightened to tell us the truth about their mysterious secret employer—Bill Sharper's correspondent.

At that same moment, we heard a knock on the door downstairs.

CHAPTER XII
The Surprising Reappearance of Bill Sharper

Two men stood on the threshold. The older was Charles, Lord Beltham's driver. He was with a young man, whom I took to be his nephew.

Seeing His Lordship, the young man lost all his composure and began to stammer and make excuses.

Lord Beltham cut him short:

"Come up here," he ordered, "and say what you have to say to Mr. Holmes. Above all, no lies, or you will regret it."

The two newcomers preceded us on the stairs and went into the room where Homes now sat in front of the Johnson brothers, with the two policemen standing guard next to them.

Charles, pointing to his nephew, spoke first:

"This here is Arthur. My nephew, to whom I lent His Lordship's car."

Holmes turned around in his chair:

"Is it true, young man? You drove His Lordship's car the night of Mrs. Murphy's disappearance?"

"No, sir," stammered the youth, almost unintelligibly.

"You weren't alone, I gather?"

"Yes, sir. I was with Harriet Meachum."

"The girl is not with you, is she?"

The young man looked at his uncle, who turned his leather cap mechanically in his fingers, and replied:

"No, sir. I didn't have time to fetch her. I knew you wanted to talk to Arthur as soon as possible, you see, and..."

"That's all right," said Holmes, returning his attention to the nephew. "At what time did you leave Scottwell Hill?"

"At half past eleven, sir."

"So you left Scottwell Hill at half past eleven in the company of young Harriet Meacham. Was she alone with you?"

"Yes, sir. You see, her parents thought that she was with her aunt and..."

"Don't start embroiling me in your petty lies. Yet, you knew that your uncle would need the car later?"

"Yes, my uncle had told me, but I thought I'd be back before the end of the fête."

"I told him not to be away for more than an hour, sir," interrupted Charles. "It's only twenty minutes from here to Southampton and..."

"Yes, I get it. At what time did you actually get back, young man?"

"Three o'clock, sir."

"How then do you explain such a delay?"

The young man blushed, turned pale and looked at us in turn.

"Did you meet someone on the road?' Holmes asked.

"Er... I don't remember..."

Charles interrupted his nephew again:

"The boy forgot to tell you something. Tell these gentlemen the story of the hat!"

We perked up our ears, interested.

"Here, sirs," stammered young Arthur, "my friend was hatless, but she became that someone might recognize her riding in His Lordship's car... So I told her to, er, borrow a lady's hat from the cloakroom—any hat, really—and put it on."

"Upon my word!" exclaimed Holmes.

"She was supposed to take care of it," Charles intervened again.

"Did that hat belong to Mrs. Murphy?"

"I don't know, sir," replied the young man. "It was covered with blue roses with white tassels on the side.

Holmes placed the shapeless wreck of a hat found on the road before young Arthur's eyes.

"It was this hat, wasn't it?" he asked.

The young man looked down and nodded.

"What happened to it?"

"Harriet was leaning out the window, and it got carried away and run over by another car."

"I see. And it was in that condition that you intended to put it back in the cloakroom?"

"My nephew is an idiot," interrupted Charles again. "When he saw that the hat was as good as destroyed, he threw it on the road on his way back here."

"Is that so?" Holmes asked the young man.

Arthur nodded.

"Now, you still haven't explained why you returned so late. What proves that you didn't kill Mrs. Murphy after dropping off your friend Harriet?"

Young Arthur, terrified, extended his right hand as if to take an oath.

"Oh, no, sir! I swear it! I'm innocent! I was with Harriet all the time, in the car. I know I've done wrong by not coming forward sooner, and I'll pay for the hat, but I'm no murderer."

Holmes turned towards one of the policeman.

"Send a man to question this Harriet Meacham in order to corroborate this young fool's testimony," he said, "but for my part, I'm convinced that he had nothing to do with Mrs. Murphy's disappearance."

The Policeman nodded and left.

My mentor then turned to Charles.

"Tell us again what happened when Mrs. Murphy came into the garage."

"It was as I told you, sur. I was hiding behind the barrel of petrol. Mrs. Murphy called for me a couple of times, then I heard someone offer her a seat in his own car."

"Why didn't she return to the living room to share her disappointment with His Lordship?"

Charles made a vague gesture.

"What do you think, My Lord?"

"I think," replied Lord Beltham, "that Mrs. Murphy didn't want to get Charles here in trouble, and seized the opportunity to grab another ride..."

Here, Lord Beltham looked sternly at Charles and his nephew.

"This, however, is where your thoughtlessness led a poor woman to a potentially abominable fate. If she has indeed been harmed, I swear you will both pay for this."

Charles and his nephew cringed.

"We will have to find who among your guests came in car, My lord," said Holmes.

"I'll ask Haxby to draw up a list," replied Lord Beltham.

Holmes then turned to look at the Johnson brothers with eyes of steel which, like a scalpel, could lay bare the most locked of minds.

"And you two claim to know nothing of this, do you?"

"Nothing, sir," said Jim.

"As God is our witness, we had nothing to do with the lady's disappearance," added Dick.

"Perhaps," said Holmes, pensive. "But we have not finished searching this house. There remains the cellar."

The cellar! The idea had already occurred to me that the brothers—or Bill Sharper—might have buried their victims there.

"Well, since we're short one man and you're here," said Holmes to the driver and his nephew, "you might as well render yourselves useful. Take a pair of shovels and follow us. You will find these tools in the storage room downstairs."

I took uncle and nephew to the room we had searched earlier. Holmes, Lord Beltham and the two brothers, followed by the policeman, followed me.

Charles and Arthur grabbed two shovels we had spotted in a corner filled with other gardening tools, and we rejoined our companions in the entrance hall, next to the small door that gave access to the garden.

There was another door, leading to a cellar, to our right; it was simply padlocked.

"The key?" asked Holmes of one of the brothers.

"Not necessary," I said, kicking the door off its hinges.

Holmes pulled a small flashlight from his pocket.

"Come along," he said to all of us as he descended a flight of stone steps.

The darkness partially hid the expression on the brothers' faces, but I could still detect their anguish.

"Move over," ordered my mentor, by shining his light sequentially on the two men and directing them to stand against the wall.

A terrible silence hung over our little party. At one point, the remaining policeman began to whistle through his teeth. I would have gladly slapped the idiot.

There were only twelve steps down. The ray of light projected by Holmes' flashlight illuminated the entire room. We saw two barrels of stout ale in the center, one half-full, the other one empty; in a corner, between two boards forming a partition, was a heap of potatoes, some of which were sprouting buds.

Holmes moved around in an excited state, stamping the compact earth floor with the wide soles of his shoes, then listening to the echo carefully.

I followed his every move. Lord Beltham stood aside, trying to guess what my mentor as up to, and somehow anticipating the horror of the drama that was about to play here.

Yet nothing seemed to indicate that anything had been buried down there.

Suddenly, Holmes' foot hit a small rock that went rolling. He saw the stone, picked it up, felt it all over the place, then called me:

"Harry."

"Yes, Mr. Holmes?"

"Do you see it?"

The electric light was lighting the small rock at close range.

"This stone is earth-incrusted," I replied. "It was recently extracted from the ground."

"Correct. So what do you conclude?"

"That a hole was dug in here," I replied.

"Excellent!"

We returned to the spot where my mentor had first made his discovery.

The light from the flashlight at first revealed no inequality or unevenness that might have betrayed a recent settlement of the wet earth then become as hard as asphalt.

Holmes had not released the stone. I saw him take it, lay it on the ground and pressed strongly with his foot on it.

The soil resisted. Then my mentor repeated the test in two or three other places without result. The fourth time, however, he smiled. Under the weight of his body, the stone had sunk completely into the ground.

"Dig here!" he told the driver and his nephew.

The shovels came down. The ground offered little resistance to their iron blades. It became obvious that the soil there had been recently disturbed:

"These are tough customers," muttered Holmes.

Then, addressing the Johnson brothers:

"You still have time to confess. Who's buried here?"

Dick opened his mouth, his teeth chattered, then he sighed deeply but said nothing. Jim remained silent, with an expression which alternated between fear and stubbornness.

Just then, Charles uttered a cry. His shovel had sunk into something soft.

Holmes lit the hole with his light and we all saw a piece of cloth, then clenched fingers.

The two men, without being given the word, pulled out a dark thing... large, cold, slimy.

It was the body of a man, now lying at our feet... a huge man, with the shoulders of an Hercules, his figure bestial and repulsive... A man still wearing a grey coat...

A single exclamation burst from all our lips:

"Sharper! Bill Sharper!"

Only Holmes remained impassive, while witnessing this incredible scene.

We had just found the body of the man whom I had suspected of being the new Jack the Ripper!

CHAPTER XIII
One Mystery Solved

When we came out of the cellar, we were all stunned.

Despite being accustomed to the frequent twists one sees in our profession, I had to pinch myself several times to make sure I was not dreaming.

Lord Beltham asked if he could be of assistance; my mentor replied that he urgently needed to send a cable to his brother and would His Lordship be kind enough to drive him into town? The master of Scottwell Hill agreed and went to fetch his car.

At last, Holmes turned towards me:

"Harry," he said, "I take it that Lord Beltham told you the story of his brother and of the animal hybrids created by that madman, Moreau?"

"Yes, he did. You think that...?"

"Yes, Harry. What we just witnessed may surprise the uninitiated minds; but for us, it was the only solution to a perfectly logical series of deductions. Bill Sharper was undoubtedly a member of that same tribe of artificially advanced apes engineered by Moreau. For all we know, he may even have been Bom-Ko's unfortunate mate, who had been left behind. Obviously, there are still a number of questions that must be answered, such as, what kept Bill Sharper returning to England? He could have just as easily quenched his blood lust in Malaysia. Who was he meeting in this house? And why was he killed?"

I was just as much in the dark as my mentor, and could offer no hypotheses.

Behind us we heard the heavy tread of the two policemen ascending with Bill Sharper's cadaver, huffing and puffing loudly. They then laid the body flat on the floor in the hallway, alongside the trunk where we had discovered the mysterious letters.

"First, we need to be certain that Sharper was an ape-man," Holmes continued, "so we need his body to be autopsied, which is why I must cable my brother at once. We can no longer leave this matter in the hands of the local constabulary..."

I looked at my mentor, wondering what he expected me to do.

"I want you to stay with the body," he explained, "and prevent anyone from examining it too closely until the men sent by Mycroft arrive to collect it. Knowing the urgency of the situation, they should be here within the hour. We shall meet at the Lyndhurst police Station later."

Holmes then ordered the two policemen to take the Jones Brothers into custody and keep them under lock and key until he could question them the following day.

By now, Lord Beltham had returned with his automobile, and in a cloud of dust, left with my mentor.

I was left alone in the sinister house to review the facts of the case.

Capturing the new "Jack the Ripper" alive and delivering him to the hangman would have certainly been something to brag about, but it wasn't to be.

Bill Sharper was dead and, with his usual pinpoint accuracy, Holmes had asked the right questions. What had he been doing aboard the *Matilda Briggs*? Who was his mysterious correspondent, "F"? And why had "F" killed him? Certainly, Sharper was himself a blood-thirsty murderer, and one might even feel tempted to congratulate the man who had thus put an end to his ghastly series of crimes. But I suspected that as not the reason for his assassination.

I concluded that only the Johnson brothers held the key to these mysteries, and looked forward to their inter-rogation.

Night was falling when I arrived at the Lyndhurst Police Station. Mycroft Holmes' men—three very non-descript operatives—had come in a van, silently collect-ed Bill Sharper's body, and left as discreetly as they had come.

The local Constable, a ruddy man named Goodfield, appeared at the door at the sound of the taxi that deposited me on the sidewalk. It was as if he had been waiting for my arrival.

We shook hands and I followed him inside, where Holmes was already waiting. I could tell at once that Goodfield treated my mentor with remarkable deference, but not without a slight note of professional jealousy.

"As I was telling Mr. Holmes," Goodfield recapped, for my benefit, "despite the rumor-mongering of a few scandal-happy reporters, we have just found Mrs. Mur-phy—alive and well."

"That is wonderful!" I said.

"Yes; her disappearance was a huge distraction," added my mentor, dryly.

"The lady is here," continued the Constable. "We took her statement earlier, but I deemed it useful to ask her to wait so you could speak to her."

"Thank you," replied Holmes. "I most certainly will."

"Now what about the two men you had me lock up?"

"The Johnson Brothers. They're involved in the murder of a, er, person whose body we found in the cellar of the house they rented on Southampton Road near Scottwell Hill."

The Constable appeared bewildered.

"A person? Who?" he asked.

"The Lyndhurst murderer, sir."

"And you know his name?"

"Yes. His name is Bill Sharper. He was a sailor aboard the *Matilda Briggs*, which my young assistant was investigating. In fact, he deserves all the credit for fingering this villain."

The assurance with which my mentor delivered the news shook the Constable.

"You say that this dead man was the Lyndhurst murderer—a murderer who was himself murdered... That is rather strange..."

"Not necessarily, sir."

"If it was not you, the great Sherlock Holmes, who was telling me this news, I confess that I would be most skeptical."

"No need to be. We will soon have the complete story," replied Holmes, "because the murderer's accomplices are now in our hands—or rather, in your cells."

"Yes, the Johnson Brothers. I see..."

"I will wish to interrogate them—but tomorrow. In the meantime, if we may see Mrs. Murphy?"

"Yes, of course," said the Constable.

He pressed a bell on his desk, and the "victim" whose corpse we had so ardently sought was immediately led in by a policeman.

She was a middle-aged, stout woman, who responded to our salutes with a friendly smile.

"These two gentlemen," said Constable Goodfield, "are the two detectives who were looking for you."

", I am so sorry, gentlemen," said Mrs. Murphy, "to have put you through so much trouble. I would never have dreamed that such a fuss would be made about my so-called disappearance. It was just stupid of me, as I realize now..."

"Still," said Holmes, "it would be good to hear the whole story from your own lips."

"Well, as you may have surmised, after leaving His Lordship's fête, I went into the cloakroom to get my coat and noticed that my hat was missing. I spent some time looking for it, without any success. By the time I got to the garage, I couldn't find my drive, and Charles, His Lordship's driver, was nowhere to be found. I suppose it was quite late, and not looking forward to this errand, he'd just retired for the night. As you can imagine, I felt pretty mortified... I didn't know what to do... Fortunately, friends of mine, Mr. and Mrs. Grey, came to my rescue by offering me a seat in their own car..."

"So you left with these friends?"

"Yes, sir. As they live in Eastleigh, I did not want to accept the offer they made to drive me back to Southampton ... Instead, they took me back to their house, where I spent the night. Mrs. Grey and I went to the same school, so I ended up staying the next day as well, which we spent reminiscing about the good old days. It wasn't until the next morning that Mr. Grey's attention was caught by the news of my so-called disappearance, and at the same time that I learned about the sorry fate of my hat—thankfully, the only victim in this nonsensical adventure."

"Nonsensical seems to be the right word," I noted, gallantly.

"Especially, sir, since I often absent myself without telling anyone," said Mrs. Murphy. "Obviously, not something I'll ever do again in the future," she added remorsefully.

"The excitement generated by the crime," said Constable Goodfield, "gave people's fertile imaginations plenty of room to embellish what was, after all, a rather ordinary situation."

"What excitement, sir?"

"The very natural emotion felt by all after the horrific crime of Lyndhurst," explained the policeman.

Mrs. Murphy blanched.

"I see. People thought that I, too, had become the victim of that sadistic madman, that vile satyr..."

"Exactly, Madam," said Goodfield. "Fortunately, you can thank Mr. Sherlock Holmes and his assistant for having pointed us in the right direction."

"I owe you two gentlemen a very big thank you," said Mrs. Murphy, with a feeling of remorse that was both charming and genuine.

"In some respects, it is we who owe you our thanks," I aid.

"Whatever for?" she exclaimed. "You speak in riddles."

"A bad professional habit, Madame," I replied. "I apologize. I shall explain. While searching for your pseudo-murderer, we found another one—a real one, this time."

"Another murderer, you say?"

"Yes, Madame, and a very dangerous one!"

"Good Heavens! Who is this monster, sir?"

"A monster indeed, Madame. He was the killer of that unfortunate woman found murdered on the Lyndhurst Commons."

"Oh!"

Mrs. Murphy, in an instinctive movement of horror, lifted her hands to her face.

"You're telling me that it's because of me that this wretch has fallen into your hands?"

"Not quite, Madame. Without your disappearance, the bandit would not be less dead, no doubt, but England would still be ignorant of the fact that it could finally breathe with relief."

"He's dead? Women have nothing more to fear from this odious character?"

"No, Madame, he is indeed dead."

Mrs. Murphy's amazement made the reveal rather enjoyable. Goodfield, too, looked rather amazed. However, much to my dismay, I noticed that Holmes stood silent, ruminating God knew what thoughts.

She repeated: "So this odious individual died?"

"Yes, Madame, and we've discovered that fact in great part thanks to you, so you see now why we—and England—owe you our thanks."

While Mrs. Murphy was pondering the enormity of this revelation, Holmes suddenly seized the opportunity to talk:

"That man, Madame, had already committed several other, equally savage crimes."

"Really?" interjected the Constable. "What other crimes? For my part, I confess I never heard of this Bill Sharper before today."

Holmes spoke slowly, weighing all his words, and his steel eyes never left the face of the Constable who, under this magnetic force, gradually stepped back.

"It's because that wretch was given a nickname, justifiably infamous in the annals of crime, a popular name quickly taken to heart by a public always eager to revel in new horrors..."

"This name, sir, please," begged Mrs. Murphy, her hands clasped.

"His name was—Jack the Ripper!"

I couldn't help frowning. I knew that Bill Sharper was not the original Jack the Ripper, even though his ghastly murders, perhaps dictated by some unfathomable biological imperative, bore striking resemblance to those committed in Whitechapel in 1888.

But then I reflected that the same political necessities that had made my mentor and his brother hide the truth twenty years before still applied. Bill Sharper, an unknown sailor, a nobody on a ship of dubious reputation, made an ideal culprit, and no one would question it twice.

"Jack the Ripper," murmured Mrs. Murphy. "So I escaped from the clutches of Jack the Ripper!"

The good piano teacher had now rewritten the whole story in her head, in order to play the heroine. No doubt she would be spending hours regaling her friends with it.

"God Almighty has done justice to that monster, ma'am," said Goodfield, "we did nothing."

Mrs. Murphy asked to leave, too perturbed, she said, to hear more. She graciously held out her hand and left.

The Constable then turned back to Holmes.

"Are you certain that the body you've found is that of Jack the Ripper, Mr. Holmes?" he inquired.

"The rest of our investigation will confirm it," my mentor replied. "No doubt there remains much more to discover. I will return tomorrow first thing to question the Johnson Brothers."

"Very well," said Goodfield. "Frankly, you are better placed than I to take the lead on that interrogation, but I am still looking forward to it very much."

CHAPTER XIV
The Search for the Truth

Friday, June 10th

The following day, Holmes and I took a quick breakfast at my hotel before rushing back to the Lyndhurst Police Station.

Constable Goodfield welcomed us before taking us to an interrogation room where the Johnson brothers were waiting, being vigilantly watched by two bobbies.

The packet of letters that we had found in the trunk was on the table, as Holmes had requested the day before.

Constable Goodfield put a pair of glasses on his nose, leaned back in his chair and staring at the two brothers, began:

"Your names?" he asked.

"Johnson," stammered brothers, and I had to intervene to establish their identity as Dick, the older of the two, and Jim.

I took this opportunity to explain briefly how my attention had been drawn to the house inhabited by the two men, the last visit made there by Bill Sharper, and the reasons which had led me to suspect a relationship between the sailor and the two brothers.

Holmes finally took the lead:

"We have here," he said, "five encoded letters signed by Sharper and sent to your address on different dates. The content of these letters still escapes us, but the signature is authentic, clear and precise."

"These letters are from Sharper?" asked the Constable.

"Yes," I said.

"We have already admitted it," said Jim, trying to articulate a defense.

"What do you think, Mr. Holmes?" asked the Constable. "Do these letters throw a light on what happened?"

"They certainly do, sir. Bill Sharper was killed inside that house that night by someone well known to the accused—someone who is likely the recipient of these letters, identified only by the letter "F." Who is this man? What connections existed between Sharper and him? These letters contain the answers to these questions."

"Were you able to decipher them?" asked Goodfield.

"No, not yet, but still, they have revealed much."

The Constable, who had been perusing the cabalistic signs spread out on the letters before him, suddenly raised his head in surprise.

"Revealed much, you say?" he repeated. "But what? For the Love of God, I can't figure out..."

"Excuse me, sir," interrupted Holmes, now slightly irritated, "but I expect these two men will help us satisfy your curiosity."

And he turned towards the brothers.

"What do you see here?" he asked Jim, pointing to the date on one of the envelopes.

"Er... June 1906..."

"And what place of origin?"

"London."

"Well, gather your memories, my boy. Wasn't a terrible crime committed that same year in June on the banks of the Thames, and its author remained unfound. The public panicked and, for the first time, someone brought up the name of that most elusive of murderers—Jack the Ripper."

"That is a big presumption, Mr. Detective."

"Perhaps. Let's look at another envelope. This one is dated a year later: Portsmouth, June 1907... Refresh your memory..."

"I don't remember..."

"I'm sure you do... Yes, another crime committed there, also in June. See, my presumption is already taking shape..."

Constable Goodfield looked at my mentor with visible great interest.

"You can't have forgotten," continued Homes, "the Glasgow attack, during which a young Irishwoman was killed. The press made much ballyhoo over it. And the date was December 1908—the same as that postmark..."

"Yeas, I see it, but it's just a coincidence."

"It is no coincidence, Mr. Johnson. All these events logically follow one another. See here: Dover, March 1909. Two prostitutes were killed, that time..."

The older brother began to shake.

"Isn't it curious," Holmes continued, "that all these letters are dated precisely from the same month and year when all these crimes were perpetrated—identical crimes, mind you?"

"Er..."

"One might suppose they're the work of the same criminal—all victims of this Jack the Ripper whose bloody signature signed each murder.

"So what, Mr. Detective?" growled Jim Johnson. "What's that got to do with us?"

"Each of these dates corresponds to a stop in England of a ship called the *Matilda Briggs*," continued Holmes, as if he was talking to himself.

"Really?"

"Yes. My information is accurate. The *Matilda Briggs* arrives; a letter is mailed; a murder is committed, almost immediately. There's some talk in the press about Jack the Ripper, then the case is closed. A year pass. The *Matilda Briggs* reappears in another English port, and the process repeats itself..."

"Good Heavens!" Goodfield couldn't help muttering.

"Each of these letters corresponds exactly to each of the stops of the *Matilda Briggs* and are precisely postmarked and dated from the port where she was calling, without exception..."

At that moment someone knocked at the door and a secretary entered and whispered a few words in Holmes' ear. This was followed by a nod of his head.

"Which brings us to Bill Sharper, who was a sailor aboard the *Matilda Briggs*," continued Holmes, as if there had been no interruption. "Now, that Sharper may have committed the murders in question during these stopovers is not the issue here. What we want to know is this: Why did he send a letter each time to your address? To whom? And what did he say?"

The brothers kept silent.

"Mr. Johnson," Holmes said, addressing Dick, the eldest of the two. "You have heard what I have just said. You know that being found an accomplice to this series of bloody crimes means a direct path to the gallows. What do you have to say for yourself?"

Jim shook his head and Dick, after opening his mouth slightly, remained silent.

"These letters were from Bill Sharper?" insisted Holmes.

"Yes, sir," sighed Dick.

"The same Bill Sharper who was a sailor aboard the *Matilda Briggs*?"

"Yes, sir."

"Why did he write to you? What did he have to say?"

Big tears slowly ran down the rough face of Dick Johnson.

"Tell us the truth, Mr. Johnson," said Goodfield, putting his hand over the brother's paw. "It'll go easier for you. Did you kill Bill Sharper?"

"No, sir."

"Who did?" asked Holmes.

The worker pointed his finger at the letters now scattered on the table.

"The recipient of the letters killed Bill Sharper?" asked my mentor.

This time, both brothers nodded.

"The best thing for you is to be forthright," said Goodfield. "Were you ignorant of Sharper's crimes?"

"He was a miserable wretch," said Dick, gasping with sobs in his voice.

"So you knew his past? His appalling crimes?" asked Goodfield.

"Oh, no, sir!" Jim protested. "Not the murders in London, Portsmouth, Glasgow and Dover... Well, we'd heard of them, of course, but this is the first time that we see Sharper accused of them! Oh! If only we'd have suspected he might have been Jack the Ripper! We thought he was a smuggler!"

"Smuggling, you say?" Goodfield interrupted.

"Yes, sir... His Captain, Arthur Beech, he's no better than Sharper."

I now understood the haste of that Beech to sail away and the little sympathy he felt for the police.

"But you really did not know that Sharper was a murderer, a sadistic monster attacking women to satisfy his atrocious passions?" insisted Goodfield.

"That, we did not know, no, sir. If we'd known it, we would have denounced him, for sure!"

Holmes spoke again:

"Excuse me," he said, "this is all very well, but I want to return to the matter of the recipient of these letters—the man who, according to you, killed Sharper—identified only in these letters as "F." Since the encrypted letters were mailed to your address, surely you must know him. Who is he?"

"We don't know, sir. That's the God-given truth."

"Yeah. We only know him as the Master."

"Why's that?"

"Because he threatened to reveal our secret to our bosses—to the police—unless we did everything he wanted."

"Yes, we're good people; we've developed a taste for an honest life... but that miserable rascal pursued us everywhere. Found us wherever we went. When he located us at Scottwell Hill, he told us that once in a while, we would receive them letters and we were to give them to him."

"Do you know what was in the letters?"

"No, sir."

"So what was this 'Master' threatening you with?"

"I'm going to tell you, sir," whimpered Dick, now a broken man. "My brother and I are escaped convicts, from Botany Bay. We'd been sentenced for armed robbery. Him, he knew us right away for what we were, despite the fact we've been leading an exemplary life. But every place we landed, he sent us threatening letters... and we were obliged to do his bidding... There was no way around it. We couldn't escape..."

"Returning to Sharper's murder," said Holmes. "It was you who lured him into an ambush for that mysterious F?"

it

"But you got rid of the body, right?"

"Well,, sir, here is how it went," said Dick, wiping his eyes with his sleeve because his hands were still trapped in the handcuffs. "The Master had become our nemesis and we were afraid of him... yes, terrorized... It was stupid, I admit it, but you know, when you're poor devils like us, it's easy to get intimidated... We wanted to live honestly, and the fear that our past would be dragged out again put us in a terrible fright. So when we saw what the Master had done—when we found Sharper's body when we returned from His Lordship's—we thought it was better to bury it in the cellar..."

"It would have been better," remarked the Constable, "to denounce your Master. His murder and his blackmailing of the two of you would have lightened the charges against you, especially in light of your past good behavior."

"That's right, sir, but we were so much afraid that we didn't think. What happened to us, I can't explain to you... We lost our heads. If the Master made good on his threats—and we knew that rascal would do it—we were lost... It would mean the destruction of all our hopes, because we're already old and we did not have the strength to run away and start all over again... So I grabbed a shovel and we dragged the body into the cellar and you know the rest... We didn't know what we were doing; we were crazy."

Dick, Jim, overcome by emotion, sank into a chair sobbing while his brother cried in a strangled voice:

Holmes approached the brother.

"I'm sure the Judge will take your confession into account," he said coldly.

Then, turning to the Constable, he added:

"I have nothing else to ask these people."

At a gesture from Goodfield, the two policemen pushed the Johnson brothers back to their cell.

After they had left, Holmes said:

"Whoever killed Bill Sharper and was blackmailing these two idiots is the man we seek. Still, I think he may have done our country a great service by ridding it of Jack the Ripper."

"Theirs was a strange story," said the Constable. "I feel we've only uncovered the tip of a vast iceberg."

"Everything is strange in our business, sir," replied Holmes, "and if all criminal cases were as easy to solve as the recent robberies at Minstead, we wouldn't have many opportunities to exercise our minds."

This was a slight to the poor Constable who had recently bungled a most ordinary case involving a series of petty crimes in the neighboring village of Minstead.

"Well, not everyone is given the chance to expose criminals like Jack the Ripper," replied Goodfield, with a bitter smile.

We left the police station in silence.

My mentor gave a shrug, then grabbed my arm and led me to the Railway station with a quick pace.

"Let's return to Baker Street, Harry," he said. "The evidence is indisputable; the conclusion inescapable... We face Fantômas!"

CHAPTER XV
Fantômas!

We didn't exchange a word in the train, or indeed until we got back to Baker Street.

Every time I tried to start a conversation, Holmes put one finger to his lips, clearly indicating that he wasn't yet ready to broach the subject.

I was left with mentally reviewing the tragic events of four years ago, when Fantômas, then posing as Dr. Garrick, had almost succeeded in killing my mentor.[8]

As we finally settled in Holmes' rooms, enjoying the wonderful tea brewed by Mrs. Hudson, I raised the subject again:

"Fantômas?"

"Who else, Harry?" replied the great detective. "We both knew that, sooner or later, we would again cross his path. I had hoped for later, but the course of events appears to have decided otherwise."

"But if Fantômas is indeed the mysterious 'F' who corresponded with, and ultimately killed, Bill sharper, why?"

"That, we don't as yet know. Nor do we know who he is and what role he plays in this strange drama."

"What made you think of him, Mr. Holmes?"

"Primarily, the presence of Lord Beltham. Do you know that this isn't the first time the two have been connected?"

---

[8] See *Sherlock Holmes vs Fantômas*, Black Coat Press, ISBN 978-1-934543-67-2.

"No, I confess I know next to nothing about Fantômas, other than what we found out during our skirmish four years ago. I asked Nick Carter afterward, but his file was desperately thin. It mentioned some kind of racket in partnership with one Etienne Rambert in 1898, which forced the man suspected of being Fantômas to flee to Mexico, and the impersonation of the detective Tom Bob, but that was it. Nothing about the man himself, nor where he came from."

"Fortunately, my brother has access to resources denied to Mr. Carter. Will you please hand me the red folder that you will find behind Goethe's *Italian Journey*, on the third shelf to your right... yes, that one... Thank you!"

I handed the folder to Holmes, who opened it slowly and, rummaging through sheaves of papers, began to offer his own narrative of the facts it contained.

"Have you heard of Rocambole?" he asked.

"Wasn't he a criminal who repented and became a do-gooder 40 or 50 years ago?" I answered. "He fought some villain who tried to steal an inheritance."

"Many villains, in fact. But yes, you might call him that," he chuckled. "He was Joseph Fipart, although that was only the name of the old crone who raised him since he was a foundling; during his youth, he served the notorious Andrea de Felipone, a master criminal, a man high in the hierarchy of the Black Coats who also operated under the alias of Sir Williams, until he turned against him and killed him. He was eventually defeated by Louise Charmet, a former courtesan known also as Baccarat, and sent to the infamous labor camp of Toulon.

"He escaped and experienced a moral resurrection, becoming, as you put it, a 'do-gooder and even earning Baccarat's support. Now posing as Major Avatar, he and

142

his companions fought a number of heinous villains and villainesses. He came to the attention of the British authorities in India when he was fighting the Thugs and was eventually caught by Sir Edward Linton, who turned out to be, as we later discovered, a first-class villain himself.

"Imprisoned in Newgate, Rocambole managed to escape and, with the help of a former thief and an Irish priest ran afoul of a scheme by Lord Palmure to steal an inheritance. Rocambole found the true heir, but was arrested again and sent back to Newgate. However, Lord Palmure's daughter, Ellen had fallen in love with him.

"Eventually, Ellen Palmure joined forces with Rocambole's friends to break him out of Newgate. Officially, we lost his trace soon after. It didn't help that the man who was Rocambole's biographer, one Pierre-Alexis Ponson du Terrail, died a year later, in 1871, while fleeing the invading German armies."

"This is all very interesting, but how does it relate to Fantômas?"

"I'm coming to that, Harry. One of the facts that M. Ponson didn't have time to relate—or perhaps chose not to?—was that Rocambole and Ellen Palmure had children—twin boys, in fact: Carl and Paul. The event was shrouded in obscurity and even my brother, with all of his vaunted resources, could only find out so much. But it would appear that Ellen gave birth to the boys somewhere in Northern Brittany, in late 1867 or early 1868. The ultimate fates of both Rocambole and Ellen Palmure are still unknown to us, but we do know that one of the boys was taken back to England by one of Ellen's former henchmen, while the other stayed in Brittany and was raised by the midwife, Anne-Marie Juve."

"Paul Juve? But isn't that the name of...?"

"The French Inspector who has fearlessly and relentlessly pursued Fantômas these last few years? Yes, it is, but I doubt that even he knows the history that I've just imparted to you. It is a strange destiny; those two boys, born to become mortal foes, one never completely defeating the other..."

"So Carl, the other boy, grew up to become Fantômas?"

"Yes. The best we could determine is that, somehow, at age seven or thereabouts, Carl was placed in the custody of Lord Edward Beltham, William's older brother. Now you know about the evil deeds of Edward Beltham? He financed Dr. Moreau's research, was the first owner of the *Matilda Briggs*, and was forced to flee England after the bloody murders committed by one of Moreau's creatures and attributed to Jack the Ripper."

"Yes, William was quite candid in telling me this shameful part of his family's history."

"What His Lordship himself may not know is that five years later, his brother, having tasted blood, began to terrorize Berlin by committing a series of murders under the alias of... Fantômas."

"So Lord Beltham was...?"

"The first Fantômas, yes. We have evidence that he was helped by his young protégé, now grown up, who at the time operated under the alias of Juan North. Four years later, he was in New York where he came to the attention of your erstwhile employer, Mr. Carter. Then, in 1899 we find him in South Africa where he joined the Boers under the alias of 'Karl Gurn.' He later betrayed them and became an artillery sergeant in the British army under the command of Lord Roberts. That's when he renewed his acquaintance with Lord Beltham and met his much younger wife, Maud, whom Beltham had married, hoping to use her royal connections to be allowed to return to England.

"In May 1900, Gurn left South Africa to return to England with the Belthams. His affair with Maud probably began on the ship taking them back to England. Two months later, Lord Beltham surprised them in bed together in their apartment in Paris; Gurn strangled him and assumed the mantle of Fantômas. The rest has been fairly well documented by a young French journalist who happens to be the son of Etienne Rambert, Gurn's murdered partner in New York.

"Now you see why the connection between the Belthams and Fantômas makes it likely that he is the one pulling the strings here."

"Yes, I do," I replied thoughtfully. "And considering how close he was to Edward Beltham, it is also likely that he would have learned the truth about the murders committed by that... that thing from Moreau's island—Bom-Ko."

"You remember how a secretary came to give me a message while we were questioning the Johnson brothers earlier?"

"Yes, of course. It slipped my mind to ask you what it was all about."

"It was a message from Mycroft, telling me that Bill Sharper's body had been autopsied and the results would be here waiting for me when I returned—which is why I was in such a hurry to get back to London."

"And...?"

Holmes grabbed a folded sheet of paper which had been lying on the table next to his armchair.

"As we suspected, Sharper was, indeed, a man-ape... A hybrid... Mycroft has already taken steps to destroy the body and falsify the results that will be sent back to the Lyndhurst Constabulary. As far as the press is concerned, the new Jack the Ripper was only a brutish foreign sailor on murderous drunken binges—and if Captain Beech is wise, he will avoid British ports in the foreseeable future."

"Pity that the whole truth can't be told" I said. "But it's just as you said, Mr. Holmes. *This is a story for which the world is not yet prepared.* Still, this wraps up the case neatly."

"Does it? I wonder, Harry... Where Fantômas in concerned, there are always wheels within wheels... Only time will tell..."

Little did I know then that we wouldn't have long to wait.

Saturday, June 11th

The next morning, as I left my hotel, having breakfasted rather late, I picked up a copy of the morning paper. As soon as I read it, I jumped into a cab and hurried to Baker Street.

I rushed into my mentor's rooms, brandishing the paper.

Holmes, who was still shaving, said:

"Ah! The news is in, I see, and the laurels are being lavishly attributed by our gentlemen of Fleet Street. I hope they didn't minimize your role in all this, Harry."

"Not quite, Mr. Holmes.," I replied, handing him the paper.

This is what he read:

A horrible crime, in all respects similar to that of Lyndhurst, just caused consternation in the charming village of Minstead. A young woman, Mrs. Neill, the wife of the local butcher, was found, her body horribly muti-

lated, on the edge of Manor Wood, just on the outskirts of the town. According to a witness, the body of the unfortunate woman was "a horrible bloody mess;" her head, almost completely severed from it, had been crushed with unprecedented savagery. There is no doubt that this new crime is the work of the same, mysterious assassin who struck in Lyndhurst last week. The Police, who claimed yesterday to have identified the Lyndhurst murderer as a sailor named William Sharper, killed by an accomplice, have now been forced to announce that the investigation is still ongoing. Perhaps Mr. Sherlock Holmes, who apparently played a part in discovering Sharper's corpse, will now be more successful in identifying the real perpetrator behind these awful crimes...

Holmes dropped the newspaper and looked at me. He had grown pale and started to pace the room back and forth, his hands behind his back, uttering a few low, unintelligible phrases.

Suddenly, he stood in front of me, crossed his arms and said:

"Where did we go wrong?"

"I don't know. I was sure Bill Sharper had done it."

"Maybe he did, and didn't... Ah! Damn Fantômas! It's all his doing, I'm sure."

"Do you think so?"

"More than ever, Harry! We rested far too comfortably on our laurels, assuming the case was all but wrapped up, when, in reality, it is only beginning..."

"What should we do?"

"We have no choice but to go back to the beginning," replied Holmes, collapsing in his chair as if he had been hit in the face. "You must return to Southampton and see what more you can find there. As for me, I must think... think..."

As my mentor sunk into depression, I left slowly, affecting a calm that I was far from feeling.

It was exactly 12:47 p.m. when I arrived at Waterloo Station looking to catch the next train to Southampton.

My mentor was right: what could I achieve by remaining in London? It was not here where I could hope to find the solution to the terrifying problem that terrorized the entire Kingdom.

To investigate a criminal case like this, it was not enough, in my opinion, to stay locked in a room, smoking a pipe, and form opinions based only on necessarily vague assumptions.

It was in Lyndhurst and Minstead where I would find the key to the puzzle.

During the journey, I reviewed all the facts in my mind, and settled on a new strategy.

A sudden shock threw me forward. The train had arrived at Southampton Station.

I returned to the Star Hotel where I was known, and where I had left the trunk with all my clothes and personal effects.

Monday, June 12th

I had spent the previous day—Sunday—in quiet meditation, preparing for the campaign to come. I had decided to discard my sailor disguise and, instead, adopt the guise of a young clergyman freshly returned from abroad. One might be wary about all kinds of people, but no one questioned a member of the clergy. A clergyman can go anywhere, from the most aristocratic castle or a rich bourgeois house to the simplest farm or the most disgusting hovel. His uniform always guarantees sympathy and even respect.

Fortunately, the costume of an Anglican priest was one of the disguises I carried in my trunk: a black frock with a narrow collar, a jacket buttoned to the chin and a pair of austere black pants, in a slightly old-fashioned cut as befitted one that had been out of the country for some time.

I also needed a hat, but there are plenty of hatters in Southampton, and I soon acquired the appropriate headgear with flat edges decorated with a beautiful cord of braided silk for a mere seven shillings.

Thus attired I left the Star Hotel and returned to Lyndhurst, where, after lunch, I checked into a modest pension owned and operated by a Mrs. Mildred Goodhope, a name which I thought was a very good augur of things to come.

Before going out, I asked Mrs. Goodhope to bring my dinner to my room that evening, claiming that I had to work on my correspondence, in order to not be disturbed by her questions. To insure her discretion, I added gravely:

"It is only by mediating upon the words of Our Lord that we can ensure to never stray from the path of virtue.

Mrs. Goodhope looked suitably impressed and accompanied me to the door, welcoming my "holy influence" on her household—especially on her husband, from what I gathered.

I walked away with a heavy sigh in the direction of Minstead. I was now ready to start on this new phase of my investigation.

CHAPTER XVI
A Stroll with Reverend Patterson

An hour later, I arrived in Minstead, and, as any self-respecting clergyman would do, I first sought out the local church, figuring that it was the logical place to gather useful information.

It was going to be a hot day; one of those when it seemed as if the sun was pouring molten lead upon the earth.

I quickly located the All Saints Church, a charming 12th century edifice located (where else?) on Church Lane. I stood a few moments in its shadow, enjoying the delightful coolness; then I headed inside and, almost immediately, was met by an imposing figure, a very large man who came towards me with outstretched hands. His cassock identified him as the local priest.

"Good morning!" he said. "You must be the new minister from Stoney Cross?"

I put on my friendliest face and replied with the greatest possible charm, affecting a slight colonial accent:

"I'm afraid not. I'm from Salisbury, Rhodesia. I've come to visit my sister in Southampton; she's been taken ill."

"I'm sorry to hear that. I'm Reverend Patterson. But surely you must have had time to explore our beautiful region?"

"Barely."

"This part of the country is stunning, my dear colleague. Here, you can't tell England from Heaven. They talk about the Isle of Wight, but it is nothing compared to the New Forest. Look around you: whichever way you turn, it's like a sea of greenery... And the air! Do you feel this balmy breeze? In our neck of the wood, folks live to be a hundred. Frankly, I'm surprised that His Majesty's government hasn't yet thought of opening up a sanatorium for debilitated children in our town."

While the good Reverend kept on praising the beauties of the New Forest, I examined him discreetly.

Despite his age, which I estimated to be in his late 60s, he was a genuine colossus, suffering from overweight, but still looking strong as an oak. His two most striking features were an abnormally large head and a pair of large feet, encased in well-worn black leather boots, pierced in places with round holes, cut to make way for painful bunions.

Suddenly, a strange idea came to me. I pictured Reverend Patterson wrapped inside a gray coat instead of a clergyman uniform, and I began to entertain some new suspicions.

Surely, it was foolish to imagine that this calm and gentle man, obviously in love with the pastoral beauty of the English countryside, could be anything but what he appeared to be—a good and honest man. Suddenly, I noticed his hands: they, too, were quite large—real slappers! Even the late Bill Sharper could not have bragged of bigger paws...

Meanwhile, Reverend Patterson continued his litany in the same soft and melodious tones, his arm outstretched toward the horizon:

"There, right behind that clump of trees, is Manor House, and behind it Manor Wood, a delightful oasis surrounded by a belt of hawthorn and privet. A wonderful corner of paradise where I often go to meditate and prepare my sermons, especially when it's hot like to-day..."

"Manor House?" I said, adding a slight stammer to my voice. "I read about it in yesterday's papers. Isn't that...?"

"Where this awful crime was committed, my dear colleague? Yes! It is especially terrifying because it's the second such murder in only a few days."

"And there's still been no arrest?"

"None at all! My personal belief is that it's the work of some vagrant who comes out at night to kill women."

"A maniac?"

"Most certainly!" replied the reverend in a troubled voice. "One of those wretches raised up by atheists, with no faith in God to stop him from sliding along the slippery slope of crime... A lunatic, surely!"

"Perhaps, but one who has certainly taken every precaution to avoid being detected."

"He could be subject to intermittent fits of madness."

"You may well be right. By 'vagrant,' I assume you don't believe it could be someone local?"

The reverend raised his arms to the Heavens:

"Oh, no, my dear colleague! Not a single soul among my parishioners could be capable of such crimes. The killer has to be a stranger, a wandering tramp, some great brute, half-man, half-beast, more likely a foreigner of some kind. I heard that Mr. Sherlock Holmes is on his trail... You may have heard of him? Well, when it comes to crime, Mr. Holmes always uncovers the wrong-doers."

"But not so far," I replied with a smile.

"One must be patient. It won't be long now. If England did not have Mr. Sherlock Holmes, I think most murderers could be assured of committing their crimes with total impunity. But fortunately, our great detective has not laid down his arms yet, and while I concede he is no longer in the prime of life, his energy and vigor are a constant source of amazement. As soon as a crime occurs, he appears on the spot as if by magic. He examines the corpse, takes a few notes, and then vanishes. And days, if not hours, later he returns, with the murderer in tow. Ah, if I were not afraid of insulting him, I'd say he were..."

"The Devil; himself?"

"Indeed," said Reverent Patterson, crossing himself. "This is only a manner of speaking, of course. My admiration for Mr. Holmes sometimes leads me to make unfortunate comparisons."

"So you are convinced that Mr. Holmes will lay hands on the culprit?"

"I'd bet a pound against a shilling."

While talking, we had arrived at a small brick house fronted by a small garden where two dusty hydrangeas barely survived in the barren soil.

"Is this where you live?" I asked the reverend.

"Oh, thank God. No!" he replied, leading me away at a brisk pace.

I had time to see a gaunt, yellow face fleetingly appear at a window on the ground floor window, as if it had been pulled away quickly.

When we were ten paces away, the reverend leaned into my ear and whispered:

"The house that you just saw has the reputation of being haunted."

"Really?" I said.

"Well, of course, I don't believe it myself, but you know how superstitious people are. That said, I have heard of some strange phenomena..."

"Such as?"

"People claim to have heard strange noises at night. And the tenant, a Mrs. Melliss, has been seen letting in mysterious individuals with sinister faces. Her neighbors say that she is a witch, and that she summons evil spirits at night, that go and possess dead bodies. This is entirely stupid, but I will tell you that I've had the opportunity of passing by several times at night, and I did hear sinister screams coming from that house..."

"Did you report it to the police?"

"Yes, but they never found anything suspicious inside. Mrs. Melliss told them she was a follower of William Crookes [9] and was free to do whatever she wanted inside her home, and desired to be left alone. Obviously, after that, she developed a grudge against me—everyone in the village is afraid of her viper' s tongue—and she started telling folks that it was I, with Dr. Smythe's complicity—who had murdered the Lyndhurst woman! She's crazy and it's better to stay away from her."

" Ah! She accused you of that?"

"Yes, and of many other things."

"Who is this Dr. Smythe you mentioned?"

"A medical scholar who engages in physiology and psychological experiments at Manor House—our local asylum, which he runs. He's friends with Lord Beltham,

[9] Sir William Crookes (1832-1919) was an English chemist and physicist who was a pioneer in the development of vacuum tubes. He later became interested in spiritualism, possibly influenced by the death from yellow fever of his younger brother Philip at age 21.

who's one of its major benefactors; as a matter of fact, I believe he is engaged to his daughter, Alice. Mrs. Melliss has accused him of being a vivisectionist, but it is more of her rubbish, of course. A month ago, she even hit him with her umbrella... It's outrageous... We must do something to rid us of that harpy. She has no respect for established institutions and she s a very bad influence in our village. Just the other day, a child I had caught for a peccadillo and whom I was lecturing made an obscene gesture at me and ran away. I chased him, and what do I see, but him entering Mrs. Melliss' house! There's no doubt in my mind that it's that shrew who incited him against me."

While vituperating, Reverend Patterson's face had become very red, and he shook his hand with much anger

This sort of village gossip held little interest for me. I looked at my watch: it was almost noon. I decided to find a pretext to leave the Reverend and have lunch at the local pub, where I might pick up more tidbits of information.

However, the worthy Reverend clung to me with the obstinacy of a cat happy to have finally found a ball of wool

Fortunately, a farmer approached Patterson, took out a crumpled piece of paper from his pocket and showed it to him.

I seized that opportunity to say a quick good-bye, then turned into the next street, and quickened my pace, feeling almost like a thief fleeing the scene of the crime.

Soon, I found myself in a wide avenue lined with trees, bordered on each side by red brick cottages. From there, I worked my way towards the center of town, where I knew I would find a pub.

All the while, I was reflecting upon what Reverend Patterson had told me. Mrs. Melliss and her mysterious visitors, and the strange noises heard in the night, might bear further investigation. Priests were not, in my experience, prone to exaggeration, and several things the good Reverend had said titillated my curiosity.

It only remained now to quickly complete my preliminary investigation of Minstead and its "actors" and then return to my lodgings in Lyndhurst to process what I had learned.

CHAPTER XVII
The Wisdom of a Tramp

I had lunch at a pub called the Trusty Servant where the languorous glances of the barmaid, which I accepted with the best evangelical unction I could summon, augured well for what I might find there.

After a slice of roast beef and a piece of Chester, all washed down with a pint of stout, I engaged in lively conversation with a garrulous old man called Charcott, who was perhaps the most talkative creature I have ever encountered.

We broke the ice after Charcott told me that I shared a vague resemblance to one of his brothers who'd died a few years earlier. Hence I was able to gain his trust and sympathy.

I steered the conversation towards the two crimes that had bloodied the region and he, too, took pride in informing me that the great Sherlock Holmes had taken an interest in the investigation and was already hot on a trail.

Like Reverend Patterson, Charcott placed the crimes squarely on the shoulders of a mad vagrant, but unlike the Reverend, he actually provided me with a suspect: a newly-arrived tramp, who reportedly had in his pocket the three shillings required by the Law and, therefore, had to be left alone by the police. However, harassed by the inhabitants of Minstead, he had finally vanished when the word had come that the police were going to detain him anyway. But instead of going by road, like any respectable tramp, he had fled into the woods.

According to Charcott, the tramp had not said anything worthy of interest while in the village. Moreover, he seemed somewhat unbalanced and sometimes rolled his eyes, looking haggard.

This mysterious tramp was, of course, of great interest to me.

After having finished my lunch, and taken leave of Mr. Charcott, I immediately began to look for the tramp, and, after three hours of relentless searching in the New Forest, I managed to find him.

He was lying on the grass in a small hollow, and seemed asleep. I approached on tiptoe and stopped about six feet away from him. By one of those fairly common phenomena that makes a person become suddenly aware that he or she is being looked upon, the tramp woke up, rubbed his eyes at some length and then, noticing me for the first time, jumped up and emitted an angry growl.

I had my hand on my gun and I was ready to use it, but the wretch remained motionless and even stepped back, looking at me with suspicion. My lack of movement in his direction appeared to reassure him because he relaxed visibly.

I could then examine him at leisure.

He hardly struck a prepossessing figure. His greasy dark hair hung in shaggy locks over his fat neck, and his rumpled beard, that had surely never known a comb or a brush, was a receptacle for a motley collection of bits of food such as bread crumbs and even fish bones. It was less a beard than a pantry!

"What are you doing here?" I asked.

"And you?" he replied in a hollow voice.

"What's your name?"

"Tom Watkins."

"Where are you from, Tom Watkins?"

A frightful grin wrinkled his poverty-ravaged face.

"From up there," he replied, pointing his finger towards the horizon in a vague northerly direction.

"From London?"

"If you'd like... London or elsewhere, does it matter? I go where I want, or are honest folks no longer free in England?"

"You do know that two very serious crimes were committed in this region?"

"Yes, I do... That's the only think they talk about... A few days ago, a policeman called Goodman..."

"Goodfield," I corrected.

"Yeah... Goodfield... He did me the honor of questioning me. You know how it goes: every time a crime's been committed, if there's a tramp about, for sure it's he that's done it! I've been used to that sort of thing, from the moment I started hanging about traveling on the roads... These policemen, what idiots they are! It's always the tramp that's done it! What asses!"

"You must admit, the circumstances are pretty damning."

"Pah! The moment a man chooses to have no fixed abode, just renting the sun God made up above, they think he's capable of anything. But, sir, I recently read in *The Times*—yes, I read *The Times* whenever I can!—that vagrants are among the citizens of our free England who commit the fewest thefts and crimes! Those who kill, plunder and steal are generally individuals with big appetites, big money needs, but we vagabonds have modest appetites... We're philosophers and know how to be content with little. As long as we have a piece of bread and a bed of straw, that's enough to make us happy. But all the others, who're slaves to the cities, barely eke out a meager living from all their sweat, they don't forgive us for living without working, oh no!"

"So you think," I interrupted, "that only tramps are honest people?"

The tramp looked me with his rheumy eyes and his patriarchal beard split in a wide smile.

"Of course! And that's what I told that Constable Goodman, er, Goodfield... Between you and I, I think the man's a famous fool! He wanted me to fess up to the murders of those women in Lyndhurst and Minstead. As I was defending myself, he insisted, probably trying to intimidate me—but that trick doesn't work with me!— using his best booming voice: 'Wretch!' he said, 'confess that it was you who slaughtered both victims!' 'And how did I do it, sir?' I asked him. 'With your bare hands!' he replied. Then, sir, I showed him my hands, my poor hands that have three fingers missing between them, and I laughed. 'You mean, with these hands?' I said, and suddenly, he looked all stupid, I can tell you that!"

And while talking, the tramp exhibited me two frightfully red, stumpy hands; one was missing two fingers, including the thumb, and the other the index.

"You see me strangling women with these?" he said, laughing. And he added, sententiously: "It's very unpleasant not to be able to use my hands, but sometimes, it can be useful. With all those pesky policemen looking for a murderer everywhere, I might have met Mr. John Ellis [10] pretty soon if I had had hands like everyone else, because those gentlemen from Scotland Yard

---

[10] John Ellis (1874-1932) was a famous British executioner for 23 years, from 1901 to 1924.

would not have failed to put me at the top of their list for those crimes. As I told you, tramps are their last recourse, when they no longer know where to turn; then they catch a vagrant, cook him up a little, brutalize him, and then hang him. But I never needed an alibi. I just had to show my hands, or at least what's left of them, and they've left me in peace."

This Tom Watkins certainly did not lack spirit, and I found him even more amusing since he told me the story of his encounter with Constable Goodfield. We always have some extra sympathy for those with whom we share the same prejudices.

I slipped half a crown in his wallet and I set out walking back to Lyndhurst through the countryside.

I was careful to check the roads, the fields, even abandoned huts, for clues; I questioned a few peasants and children, but I found nothing of interest.

It was getting towards the end of the afternoon and, as I felt tired, I sat on a grassy hillock and, after lighting my pipe, I began to think.

Suddenly my attention was caught by a fairly common sight; one that excited my curiosity as a detective and aroused my suspicions.

Before me, to the left, was a large gray wall, behind which there must have been a small elevation of the ground, because, from time to time, I saw the head and shoulders of a man pass by.

Then, the man came to lean over the edge of the wall, and, having noticed me, showed me his fist, fiercely uttering insults that I could not hear.

I probably would not have paid attention to the stupid actions of an unknown peasant, if there hadn't been something unusual in that character who was gesticulating furiously while continuing to hurl insults at me.

I looked at him more carefully.

He had a huge hydrocephalic head sitting on top of the shoulders of a colossus, with hands as large as a beater—and he wore a gray jacket!

If I hadn't seen Bill Sharper's corpse with my own two eyes, I could have sworn it was the sailor of the *Matilda Briggs* who stood there, before me, snarling and angry, with his beastly face, mouth and thick lips...

And it was suddenly as if a veil had been torn away... What at first had been a mere supposition became almost a certainty. I remembered the description given to Holmes and me by Mrs. Porter in Baker Street:

" ...His huge back... his thick legs... He wore no hat, and he was dressed all in gray..."

The *Man in Gray*, the monster with the huge head, was he the same person that now stood before me?

Could it be true? Minstead was close to Lyndhurst. He could have run undetected through the woods. He only had to jump that wall and he was in the countryside...

Without worrying about the giant in gray who continued to insult me, huffing and puffing like a seal—another trait mentioned by Mrs. Porter—I walked to the end of the wall, where I could see, between two massive columns garlanded with ivy, the imposing arch of a wrought iron gate.

Bolted to one of the stone pillars was a brass plate that read:

MANOR HOUSE – LUNATIC ASYLUM – JOHN SMYTHE, M.D.

CHAPTER XVIII
A New Trail

This time, I thought, *I'm truly holding the thread that will lead me to the new Jack the Ripper!*

The killer had to be that poor, demented lunatic, badly monitored at night, who'd climbed over the asylum wall and randomly gone after women. The insane, bestial face that had grimaced at me was undoubtedly that of the murderer we'd been seeking.

However, I couldn't afford to rush to judgment and, through a bold but foolish move, risk compromising my investigation. I had to get inside the asylum, talk to Dr. Smythe, gather the proof I needed and then... then, we would see!

It was about five o'clock in the afternoon. I decided to abandon my clergyman's disguise, and reveal myself under my true identity. My disguises were always carefully planned so that I could switch them in an instant by simply reversing the clothes or folding some items under my shirt.

I always favored neutral colors, because a detective shouldn't wear vibrant fabrics that would attract the eyes like a semaphore flame unless, of course, he wishes to be noticed. This is why I wore gray or beige suits.

It took me barely a minute to turn my cassock into a suit, and wipe the makeup I had worn to imitate the tan of a colonial from my face. Using makeup well is a complex art that only actors and true detectives seem to have mastered to perfection. There really is no need for fake mustaches or dark glasses to distort a face. A real detective can manufacture the sardonic look of a Cockney gentleman, the bewildered look of a cow which sees an automobile for the first time, or the jaded and indifferent gaze of the aged civil servant behind his desk at will.

I had moved around without being recognized, but it was now time to revert to my true identity. Having finished the job, I put the small oval mirror and the few tubes of makeup back in my pocket and got up.

I shook my "new" gray jacket and trousers so they hung more naturally, and then I forcefully pulled the iron chain at the gate that was attached to a brass bell affixed beneath a small glass awning.

The bell made a deafening sound, somewhat comparable to that of Big Ben, sending sound waves all the way across the paved courtyard that separated the smaller adjacent units from the main building.

Another bell rang three times, in the distance, and a tall man with short arms but very long legs, looking not unlike a kangaroo, came out of one of the smaller buildings.

When he was near the gate, he looked at me with a superior air, without responding to my salutation, and merely asked for the purpose of my visit.

"I wish to speak to Dr. Smythe," I replied with a pleasant smile.

"Do you have a letter of introduction?"

"No, but give him my card and I'm sure he'll see me immediately. I'm a friend of Lord Beltham."

I slipped a business card and half a pound into the orderly's hand through the bars of the gate.

His face brightened immediately and he finally responded to my earlier salutation. Then, he opened the gate, saying:

"Come in, sir. I will communicate the news of your presence here to Dr. Smythe."

My half-pound had had its desired effect, I thought, and I now had an ally in the place.

One of the failures of the police, and even of detectives, is often to be too parsimonious; they think that their very presence must open all doors, and instead of seeking allies amongst domestics and menial clerks, they take on the airs of gentlemen, which only alienate the sympathies of servants, and stifle their confidences. I, on the contrary, was always very generous with them, because I know from experience that they are never immune to the appeal of a beautiful gold coin.

My guide led me through the courtyard; then we went up white marble steps that led to a hallway, on the walls of which were pinned large yellow health department posters.

"Is Dr. Smythe in his surgery?" asked the employee to a supervisor who was pacing the hallway with a melancholy face.

"Yes. What do you want with him?"

"This gentleman desires to speak to him."

And he handed the card I had given him to his colleague.

Five minutes later, I stood in front of Dr. Smythe, the director of the Manor House Lunatic Asylum.

He was a tall, handsome, dark-haired man in his late 30s or early 40s, with burning, black eyes framed by round glasses. A think mustache decorated his upper lip.

We shook hands firmly, after which he invited me to sit across from him.

"A gentleman detective," he said, looking at my card. "I confess to some bewilderment here. Are you here to investigate a complaint against my establishment? If so, I shall tell you right away that it's slander, yes, pure slander. I run a model asylum here, with all the modern improvements one would expect from a top facility. Since I took over from my predecessor, I have only received praise from the medical community..."

"So you didn't set up this asylum?"

"No. This facility was originally set up by the renowned Dr. Lionel Prospero McDuff, who passed away in December 1908. I'd had the privilege of working alongside him, and I naturally took over after his unfortunate passing. I'm the one who decided to move the place to Minstead, because I grew up nearby, and I thought the rural setting would be good for our patients."

"Where were you before?"

"In Glasgow."

"Did Dr. McDuff experience any problems there?"

"What kind of problems?"

"I don't know... Violent patients... Escapes..."

"Not as far as I know, no. I'm well aware that I have enemies here, who miss no opportunity to denigrate me and my facility. I am accused of being too good to my patients, treating then with too much kindness, but my methods have produced excellent results. Most lunatics are often far more reasonable than people suspect. I try not to antagonize them. I'd go as far as to state that some here hate me because I try to heal patients that were committed primarily because they were a burden to their families, or an obstacle to their greed. But I do not care; I do my duty, and nothing but. We must pity the innocent and treat them kindly, said Dickens. I follow to the letter this wonderful quote from one of England's most illustrious writers..."

I tried to get a word in edgewise, but Dr. Smythe would not be stopped and continued with renewed animation:

"Yes, kindness is everything, Mr. Dickson. If you only saw the wonderful results I achieve here! My way of dealing with these poor hapless souls may seem bizarre to a layman, but when my colleagues in the medical community saw my results—bringing peace to the furious and joy to the depressed—they started to take me seriously. I have gotten rid of the cold showers, the whips, the straitjackets, and the electroshocks. I'm content to walk amongst my patients, who may be a little mischievous occasionally, but in reality are not much worse than many men and women deemed to be sound of mind..."

"That's wonderful!" I exclaimed, trying to halt his flow of eloquence. "I understand that you have received the support of Lord Beltham—and his daughter."

"I see that you have been listening to the local gossip," he said, smiling. "But in this instance, the gossip happens to be correct. As I mentioned I grew up around here, and the first thing I did after moving the asylum to Minstead was to call on his Lordship to beg for his largesse in order to improve my facility. I don't mind telling you that he has been generous, very generous indeed. During one of my visits, I met his only daughter, Alice. She is a sweet, romantic soul, with a big heart, and I think my approach to my patients—kindness—touched something in her. We are now engaged, and plan to be married before the year is over."

"Congratulations!" I said. "As it happens, I have had the pleasure of meeting His Lordship during my investigation..."

And here, I briefly told him of the events of the past few days and outlined the purpose of my visit.

He listened, seriously, and when I finished, said in a solemn tone:

"Mr. Dickson, it is impossible that the 'Man in Gray' whom you seek is one of my patients. I have read about the crimes you mentioned in the newspapers; they were both committed at night. But all my patients are locked up after 8 p.m."

"Perhaps one of them was able to trick your orderlies and remain hidden in the park and jump the wall after the lights were out?"

"Impossible. We do a roll call every night."

I thought it pointless to insist. Obviously, I wasn't going to get anything useful by challenging him that way. Instead, I chose flattery.

"Well, it was worth asking," I said, with a dismissive wave of the hand. "Leave no stone unturned, eh? But I confess to being very impressed by everything you've told me. In my business, we're often called on to deal with unbalanced minds. Would you do me the great favor of giving me a tour of your asylum? It would be of great benefit to me."

I thought I saw a tiny flicker of annoyance when he heard my request, but I might have imagined it. In any event, he could hardly turn me down and, indeed, beamed a proud smile at me, saying"

"I'll be delighted, my dear fellow. The more publicity you give my methods, the greater their influence. You'll see with your own eyes what can be achieved with humanity and kindness, instead of cold showers and whips. Come with me and I'll show you my patients."

He put a small cap of green velvet on his head, took a bunch of keys from one of his desk drawers and led me to the main building, located a hundred yards from his office.

At the end of a long hallway, he opened an iron door and politely stood aside to let me pass.

"We are in the ward of the megalomaniacs," he explained.

There were men with eyes staring into emptiness, who walked somberly in their grey uniforms, their heads held high, their arms crossed or behind their backs, like generals on the eve of a battle.

Dr. Smythe identified some of these unfortunates and I learned that these residents with delusions of grandeur included four Napoleons, two Wellingtons and, oddly one George Washington.

Then we went into another ward, that of the congenital idiots, then another with a variety of disorders, including pyromaniacs and neurasthenics, and we finally arrived at the ward of the violent patients suffering from hysteria and dementia.

"Wait here," said Dr. Smythe.

And he cautiously opened a solid oak door.

We found ourselves in a courtyard surrounded by stone walls, where a dozen individuals were engaged in various disorderly antics. Some behaved like monkeys, rolling on the ground, scratching spitting and foaming at the mouth; others looked decidedly more threatening, gesticulating wildly, uttering meaningless sentences, in which the same words were repeated several times.

A massive guard, armed with a whip, walked quietly among these restless souls.

"Well," I said, "it would seem that in here your method of kindness is tempered with strength."

"Ah, ah!" he said with a forced laugh, "you say that because you saw the orderly's whip, but rest assured, he never uses it, it's just to scare the patients when they're tempted to behave badly, isn't that right, Mr. Tripp?"

"Yes, Doctor," replied the orderly, concealing his whip behind him.

But judging from the look Dr. Smyth gave him, I guessed that Mr. Tripp would be roundly reprimanded later for having failed to conceal that weapon from an outside visitor, thus giving the lie to the humanitarian theories of the director of this so-called model Asylum.

Dr. Smythe seemed to be looking for someone. His face reflected a deep concern and it was in a trembling voice that he asked the orderly:

"Mr. Tripp, where is Bumpkin? I do not see him. Did you lock him up in the shed for some misconduct?"

The orderly looked around in bewilderment, then replied with embarrassment:

"Er, I may have left for a moment... He's undoubtedly taken advantage of my absence to go back to his room... Or go out... Wait! I'll fetch him!"

And he left muttering:

"Damned Bumpkin! Always something with him... but I swear I'll make him pay this time!"

With the orderly gone, the madmen all around us starting to gather around us and hurl the foulest insults. Some even threatened us with their fists and I could see a risk of their actually jumping us.

"Fear not," said Dr. Smythe. "I'll disarm them with kindness."

At that moment, a madman kicked him hard in the legs, causing his green velvet cap to fall. Another lunatic grabbed it and began tearing it with his teeth.

"Come, my friends! Come!" cried Dr. Smythe. "You know that I do not like these sorts of jokes... If you continue, I'm warning you: I will get angry."

The madmen stepped back, but still looked threatening:

"Hou! Hou!" shouted the Director, raising his arms.

A clamor of revolt issued from the lunatics and I saw that we would soon be attacked by that howling band.

Fortunately, Mr. Tripp came back, pushing before him with blows of his whip a Herculean creature whose clothes were smeared with mud. I realized "Bumpkin" was the same person I had seen on the other side of the wall. From time to time, he tried to punch the orderly, but every time, Mr. Tripp avoided his blows by nimbly stepping aside.

As he approached, the other lunatics fled, terrified, but the newcomer rushed at them and began to beat them up, accompanying each of his blows with strange, foreign words, from a language I did not recognize, but which sounded vaguely Asian.

He then began to stomp furiously the body of one of the madmen whom he had thrown to the floor.

Mr. Tripp administered five lashes of his whips to the Hercules, driving him away, while Dr. Smythe helped the victim of that terrible pugilist to get back up.

"This is a very dangerous individual," I said to the director.

"Him? No, on the contrary, Bumpkin is the gentlest of creatures."

"Really?"

"Don't pay attention to this very unusual behavior. The poor devil has bad days, like the rest of us. Obviously, something must have upset him, but after an hour in the shed, he'll be as calm and reasonable as you and I."

The spectacle that had just happened before my eyes made me doubt the Director's words. Bumpkin was a dangerous brute. The way he had stomped his opponent while the man was on the ground denoted an unprecedented ferocity, and one could expect anything from such an individual. His thick, sensual lips, his shining, fierce eyes, his bulging neck, betrayed a creature that was the prey of his basest passions.

This man was crazy, it was clear to me, and contrary to what Dr. Smythe had claimed, I thought he suffered from those sadistic intermittent episodes which Lombroso [11] called "carnal maniacs," like the despicable Sergeant Bertrand,[12] who experienced horrible thrills by maiming his victims with his teeth and crushing their bones with his hands.

At last, I thought I had found the assassin, but there were still many things left unclear. If Dr. Smythe was correct, how had he escaped from the Asylum? And if someone had let him out, then why?

---

[11] Cesare Lombroso (1835-1909) was an Italian criminologist and physician, founder of the Italian School of Positivist Criminology, often referred to as the father of criminology.

[12] Sergeant François Bertrand (1823-1878), known as the Vampire of Montparnasse, was arrested in 1849 for necrophilia. Between the summer of 1848 and March 1849, a series of bodies were exhumed and found severely mutilated in cemeteries of Paris. On 15 March 1859, Bertrand admitted himself to the Val-de-Grâce hospital with gunshot wounds. A gravedigger at Montparnasse Cemetery overheard the news about Bertrand's injury, and realized that he must be the same person hit by his colleague's booby trap. One of Bertrand's surgeons obtained a full confession. Bertrand was arrested and sentenced to one year in jail. In his later life, he worked as clerk, mailman, and lighthouse keeper, and died on 25 February 1878. Bertrand's case prompted renowned alienist Joseph Guislain to coin the term "necrophilia."

I needed more time—and more proof.

So I said good-bye to Dr. Smythe and returned to Mrs. Goodhope's pension in Lyndhurst to spend the night and plan for the next day of my campaign.

CHAPTER XIX
Toby to the rescue!

Tuesday, June 13th

The next day, I decided to return to the Trusty Servant for lunch. It wasn't a bad pub, and I was hoping that the helpful Mr. Charcott would be there to provide me with more information about Dr. Smythe's Asylum.

I felt in my bones that, this time, it was only a matter of time before I unmasked the mysterious Bumpkin as the Man in Gray. Yet, his connection with Bill Sharper, the *Matilda Briggs*, and the ever-elusive Fantômas—assuming my mentor had been correct-still escaped me.

Bumpkin was a colossal force of nature. Against a creature like him, my revolver might prove as useful as a pea shooter. Worse, if I shot him dead, I might be accused of having murdered a lunatic, and face dire consequences... Therefore, if my plan was to succeed, it all had to be done within the confines of the Law.

The best thing to do was, I believed, to monitor Bumpkin, try to catch him *in flagrante delicto*, or failing that, to apprehend him on his return to the Asylum.

It was obviously easier said than done, especially since my duty as detective forbade me from letting that brute kill another hapless victim if I could prevent it.

I was still thinking about this dilemma when I arrived at the Trusty Servant. There, an idea suddenly popped into my head.

I noticed a huge mastiff chained in the pub's courtyard. If I could take that dog with me, I thought, I could save the next victim!

It was indeed the dream auxiliary, because Bumpkin would certainly fail to kill his prey if he was busy defending himself against a mastiff of that size!

While I was pondering how to best "borrow" the dog, from the corner of my eye, I spied a huge black figure whose flickering shadows danced along the hedges.

It was Reverend Patterson, walking in my general direction.

As the path was narrow, I stepped aside politely to let him pass. He gave me a furtive glance, raised his hand to his hat and muttered a few words I didn't understand.

He had not recognized me, of course. What connection could there be between me and the friendly young South African priest that he had met the day before.

I bowed, smiling, he did the same, and we continued on our separate ways.

His curiosity was, after all, natural enough; outsiders were rare in Minstead and any new figure was bound to attract suspicion.

Still pondering my next course of action, I walked down the road and found a street lined with gardens, which ended in a small place called Green Crescent, the center of which was a crumbling bandstand.

Suddenly, I recognized the silhouette of Mr. Charcott sitting on a bench, next to another man; both seemed engaged in lively conversation.

I approached and tapped him amicably on the shoulder, as if he were an old friend. I didn't expect him to recognize me, of course, but I quickly introduced myself, explaining that I'd been using a disguise to investigate the murders.

They were both amazed, as they had never encountered a private detective before.

Mr. Charcott introduced me to the other man, Mr. Fass, retired from the Army, a little man with a pointy head and square shoulders.

"You're right to snoop around, Mr. Dickson," said Fass. "You should look at that Dr. Smythe. When one is engaged in experiments on living animals, one is capable of doing the same with humans. These vivisectionists have no hearts. It's clear he created a monster!"

"What's clear, Fass," replied Charcott, "is that you've attended one too many of Miss Melliss' séances. That crazy old woman wants nothing more than Smythe's head mounted on a wall."

"Not at all," replied the little man quickly. "True, I attend her séances, but I don't need anyone to help me form my own opinion."

"What does Miss Melliss have against Dr. Smythe?" I inquired.

"Manor House used to belong to her family," started Charcott. "They fell on hard times and she was forced to sell. She never forgave the Doctor for buying it."

"Well, that's true," conceded Fass. "But I don't think it has anything to do with the basis for her accusations."

"What basis?" said Charcott. "The spirits who speak through her turning tables?"

"No, no..." said Fass, frowning. "Although sometimes the spirits can teach us some very curious things... I simply proceed by deduction."

"Like the great Sherlock Holmes, then?" said Charcott, laughing.

"If you want..."

"What are your deductions then, Master Fass?" said Charcott, still laughing. "Enlighten us, please."

The little man was not intimidated; he stood up to his opponent. He crossed his arms over his chest, then uttered in a nasal voice that seemed to come from a phonograph:

"My deductions? They are very simple. When a man has committed a crime, what does he do? He hides, doesn't he? Ever since this thing began, Dr. Smythe has been staying shuttered inside his hospital. We used to see him driving around in his motorcar, taking Miss Alice to this or that function, but he's virtually disappeared since the day that woman was found murdered on the Lyndhurst common!"

"Well deduced, Master Fass," said Charcott, smiling, "but you seem to forget that the reason you haven't seen much of Dr. Smythe since the Lyndhurst murder is simply that he is a busy man. He was at Lord Beltham's last Wednesday..."

"Yes, that is true," I said, cutting in.

"...And he was among the first to talk to the police after they found the second body last Saturday. Your reasoning does not hold up. Besides, what would Dr. Smythe have to gain from all this?"

"I don't know," grumbled Fass. "Maybe he's experimenting anew on his patients..."

"Your hatred blinds you, my friend. If this is the sum of all your deductions, let me tell you, they do you no honor."

"We'll see," said the little man looking slyly at his interlocutor.

At that moment, a village woman carrying a basket of groceries stopped to take part in the conversation.

"I heard that Mr. Sherlock Holmes himself is on the case," she whispered, as if someone might have cared about our discussion. "Constable Goodfield isn't too happy about it, according to one of my friends in Lyndhurst."

"You're a private detective," said Fass. "Do you work for Mr. Holmes?"

"Not for, exactly," I replied. "More like with him. But yes, I am collaborating with him on this case."

"Oh, that is quite extraordinary," said the lady, whose name was Mrs. Green, in a squeaky voice.

"Have you found the murderer yet?" asked Fass, rather bluntly.

"Not yet, but we're following several promising leads," I said.

Mrs. Green continued unmoved:

"The great Sherlock Holmes on the trail of the murderer in Minstead. If only my Alfred had lived to see this!"

We all nodded sententiously, this being something about which we could all agree.

Then Mrs. Green went away with Fass, and I decided to invite Charcott to lunch at the Trusty Servant. Since he seemed to be a friend of the Landlord, I thought he might help me to "borrow" the dog.

He heartily accepted and we walked back to the pub, all the while making idle talk about the recent appointment of Sir Charles Harding as Viceroy of India and Scott's expedition to the south pole.

When I had finished my meal, I regretted having invited Charcott, because he was a real chatterbox. His memory—or his imagination—were never at fault, nor was there any interruption in his speeches. It was hard to a get a word in edgewise and any attempt at halting his flow of words would be met with an authoritarian gesture of his hand inviting me to let him continue.

Realizing that I would not get rid of him as long as I sat next to him, I suddenly stood up, feigning uneasiness, and went to the bathroom after having, in a doleful voice, wished him a good afternoon.

After a while, I heard him leave and I could safely come out from my hiding place. I sat in a large armchair covered with faded velvet and I finally enjoyed some peace.

I thought of Bumpkin and I could easily remember the image of the giant stomping on his opponent, uttering wild howls, and, by a natural association of ideas, I pictured him assaulting the two unfortunate victims of Lyndhurst and Minstead in the same manner. I could hear their bones crack, and see the monster knead their bloody flesh with his huge hands. I pictured the murder scene in my mind... Bumpkin there, lurking in the grass, his beastly eyes alert, his chest heaving, shaking his fists convulsively... Suddenly, in the pale moonlight, a shadow loomed... then came into the light... A woman... The creature jumped silently, throwing himself upon his victim, striking her in the blink of an eye... Then, standing over her body, choking her, pitiful groans coming from her mouth... Then, there would have been a dull sound, similar to a stick breaking, and the deed was done, but the ignoble butchery went on... Later, a quick run through the woods... the enormous silhouette reached the asylum's wall, and nimbly went over it...

More than ever, I needed an ally if I were to have even a prayer of defeating that monster!

I got up and went to the bow window, left ajar, that looked into the courtyard. I could make out the dark shape of the dog, resting in the shade.

Just then, someone walked by and the dog immediately rose up, barking furiously and threateningly.

Another window opened, that of the kitchen, and I heard the voice of the Landlord saying:

"Shut up, Toby! Rest!"

The dog growled, ambled back his doghouse, where he turned for a moment, then suddenly he fell to the ground and remained motionless and silent.

This mastiff would indeed make the ideal assistant for my nocturnal expedition—if I could take him out of the pub.

I stayed a while leaning against my window, and then I began to whistle softly.

Toby, who was not chained, moved out of his doghouse and came to the window growling.

I took a few sugar cubes placed in a saucer beside a jug of water on the counter and I threw one to the animal.

The dog looked at the cube for a few seconds, then began to chew it with a terrible sound of jaws crunching.

I gave him a second cube, which he caught in mid-air, and a third that he missed. As I stopped, Toby began barking and unceremoniously put his huge paws on the window sill.

This time, he was emboldened enough to take the sugar cubes from my hand, which he did in a very delicate matter, and I gently patted his head, saying softly:

"Good dog, Toby! You're a good dog!"

I felt my hand the wet and warm tongue of the good animal.

I had made a conquest of Toby; there remained now for me to lead him out of his home after sunset.

At night fall, I returned to the pub, stepped slowly to the back fence, picked the lock, and slipped into the yard.

This time, the dog began to bark and I thought that he was going to wake the Landlord up, but a new cube of sugar instantly calmed the anger of my new-found ally.

I stroked Toby again and peace was between us. I went back out; he followed me.

I was wearing a dark coat, a dark hat and my revolver was in my pocket, as well as a supply of sugar cubes as inducements for my auxiliary.

In fact, I gave him one to make sure of his complicity as I closed the back fence behind us.

As soon as we reached the outskirts of Minstead, walking towards Manor House, Toby began to frolic, uttering little yelps of joy.

He was definitely a good dog, but I would have preferred it if he had been a little more silent.

When we were at a distance that I judged to be optimal, I called him to me and pointing to the woods that led to the asylum, I said in a low voice:

"Seek Toby! Seek the monster!"

The animal jumped into the bushes, plowed the land with his nose and came back to me with a friendly yelp.

That's all I needed to know. At my order, Toby would attack anyone, man or beast. I petted him some more and sent him out again.

With a good Browning in my pocket, and this dog by my side, I didn't fear anyone, and Bumpkin, despite all his bestial savagery, would fall before me.

I had reached the edge of the woods and the Moon, which had just come out from behind the clouds, cast a pale, velvety light upon the countryside.

Eleven strokes rang at the Church, then, slowly, other neighboring churches did the same.

Toby was running by my side; sometimes, he was going at full speed, as if I'd thrown him a ball; at other times, he wandered into the brush where I heard him digging and sniffing loudly.

I decided to keep him on a leash and I passed a rope through the ring of his collar. I wanted to be sure he would not compromise my expedition.

Arriving in the middle of the fields equidistant between the gray wall of the Lunatic Asylum and the New Forest, the dark mass of which blocked off the horizon, I sat on the grass, taking Toby between my legs, and waited.

After an hour, my four-legged companion, who was bored, began to bark plaintively.

I stroked him and he fell silent again, but, in the moonlight, I could see his big white eyes, looking at me as if to say: 'Is that why you brought me here? You would have done better to leave me at home. What are we doing here? Come on, get up and let's go!'

The night was already well advanced and I had not noticed anything suspicious yet. Nobody had crossed the fields. The locals had become wary now, preferring to make a two miles detour rather than going through the place where the terrible crime had been committed.

Already, I despaired at the thought that, in all likelihood, I would have to keep watch every night for weeks, months perhaps, without being more advanced than the first day. And those long watches would eventually attract the attention of people of Minstead...

I was not the end of my troubles. However, I could not hire a woman to accompany me every night and bait the monster!

I had to once again count on the luck that, in my detective career, had so often favored me.

Wednesday, June 14th

The sun would soon appear.

A wan light rose gradually to the east, and the cold that always accompanies the dawn fell on my shoulders like a rain of icy shards.

Poor Toby was cold, too, and I felt him shudder against me.

I rose to leave when, suddenly, he growled furiously.

I tried to calm him, caressing him, but he was making desperate leaps and I had great difficulty in keeping hold of him.

Obviously, he had smelled something.

A few seconds passed. Toby still continued to growl and pull on the rope that I used as his leash.

Suddenly, a figure stood in the fields, about twenty meters from where I was.

I thought I recognized Bumpkin. It was the same build, the same massive and rounded shoulders, the same long, gnarled arms. This silhouette seemed huge, larger than life, but I attributed it to the fog that surrounded it and which, as we know, has the property of magnifying objects.

Instinctively, I pulled my gun out of my pocket and waited, still holding Toby, who kept growling furiously.

The giant now stood motionless between two clumps of trees where he stood out even more clearly on the horizon.

He seemed hesitant.

Maybe he had heard Toby and was worried?

At one point, I saw him fall, then straighten up suddenly and disappear into a thicket. I heard the sound of rustling leaves, the cracking of branches, then there was silence, gloomy, mysterious.

Had he seen me? No, that was impossible, because the place where I stood was surrounded by thick bushes, rendering me virtually invisible in the dim light of dusk.

I got up and let Toby lead me hurriedly in the direction where my target had disappeared.

Suddenly, I heard a sinister cry, a harsh and terrifying scream, and almost immediately, I saw two black shapes stand out on the horizon, then melt immediately in the dark trees.

This time, I no longer hesitated.

I thought that Bumpkin had found a new victim and was in the process of attacking her.

I unleashed Toby who flew like a bird and I started running towards the direction from which the scream had come.

The two shadows had reappeared and, this time, I clearly distinguished a fleeing man, pursued by the monster.

The unfortunate victim ran madly with astounding speed, as if he had wings. But his pursuer was no less quick. Soon he would catch up with him.

I saw two great arms rise and fall on the victim, who rolled on the ground, issuing another scream, even more terrifying than the first.

Toby was already on the monster; he bit him with great gusto, snarling and growling and clawing.

Having reached the group, I aimed my gun at the creature, which I saw only confusedly, and twice I pulled the trigger.

I heard a scream, saw the embrace of the monster loosened; he'd released his victim.

He leaped back and disappeared into the woods.

Toby was going after him, but not wanting to risk his life, I called him back. He came trotting back to me, obviously very proud of his bravery.

"Are you hurt?" I asked the man lying on the ground.

"No... it's nothing," he replied. "Go after him!"

By the light of the Moon, I saw that it was Charcott. What on Earth was he doing there?

"He can't be very far," he continued. "Kill him...You must kill him, Harry!"

And then, to my amazement, Charcott pulled off a wig and did something to his face, and at last I saw who he truly was...

Sherlock Holmes!

CHAPTER XX
Am I going mad?

As I stood gaping, dumbfounded, Holmes shouted furiously at me, mopping the blood dripping down his face with his handkerchief:

"Go after him, Harry! Kill him before he gets away!"

I jumped into the thicket, revolver in hand. In front of me, I heard the cracking of branches, and I could quite clearly see a huge gray thing that moved furiously, trying to make its way through the brambles.

I fired two more shots, and I suppose I hit him, because a howl of pain immediately arose.

I continued my pursuit, believing at every turn that I would catch up with the monster, but after nearly half an hour, I had to finally admit to myself that he had escaped, and I had lost his trail.

Out of breath, embarrassed, my legs trembling, I returned to where I had left Sherlock Holmes.

He was sitting, trying to bandage his left wrist with his handkerchief, Toby at his side, delivering what I'm sure he thought were helpful licks.

On seeing me, he rose painfully, and then, threw his good arm around my neck and embraced me warmly, murmuring with emotion:

"Thank you, Harry, thank you. I would have been lost without you!"

We had last seen each other in his Baker Street flat, and now, here we were, both on the battlefield. He was wounded: he had a hideous head wound and his right wrist was likely broken—but he was alive! Once again, I admired the courage of this man who had not been afraid to risk his own life to find the monster that terrified the country. He truly was a hero, and his blood-spattered face gave him a look both fierce and imposing.

He wasn't just a man who made deductions in the safe comfort of his rooms, but a man of action, who never shirked his duty—a real detective in the fullest sense of the word, and I swore to be someday worthy of him.

"He's escaped?" he asked in a heartbroken tone.

"Yes," I replied, "but I think I hit him twice, perhaps three times. With bullets in his body, he won't go far, for sure. In any event, I have a good idea where he might go. I can catch up with him later. I should take you back to Minstead..."

"Yes. Let's return to the village. You can call for reinforcements from the police and I, during that time, will heal. Because I want to be there when you arrest that monster!"

"Is that wise? He broke your wrist."

"No. I believe it to be merely dislocated. Give me a little time to regain my wits and I'll be good as new. Ah! That creature is of prodigious strength, Harry! He surely would have crushed me like a child if you hadn't showed up."

"Didn't you have your gun?"

"I did, but the monster jumped on me before I could use it, and it fell to the ground during our battle."

"Were you able to identify him?"

"Sadly, no. He was frighteningly fast and had me in his grip before I could look at his face. I hope you mortally wounded him, Harry! We may not have the satisfaction of delivering him to justice alivr, but at least we'll have freed humanity from that blood-thirsty creature. Come on, help me and let's go back to Minstead."

While I helped my mentor shed the last remnants of his disguise, Holmes told me smiling:

"You never suspected me of being Charcott, did you? I confess that I had some fun at your expense, Harry. I had recognized you as that South African priest wandering about, asking questions, so I thought I'd play the same trick on you. I hope you aren't mad at me?"

"Not in the least," I replied good-humoredly. "I can but hope to someday equal your skills as a master of disguise."

I offered my arm to Holmes for him to lean on, and we headed slowly back towards Minstead, followed by Toby.

On the way, my mentor asked me several questions about what I had learned, which I answered in full and with as many details I could recall.

By the time we reached the small road leading to Green Crescent, Holmes asked me, looking me right in the eyes::

"So, Harry, according to you, who is the killer?"

"The lunatic known as Bumpkin, from Manor House. What I haven't figured out yet is the why."

"We always assumed madness was sufficient reason to explain these murders."

"Yes, but I don't think so anymore.

"What next?"

"As you proposed., let's ask Goodfield to send us two strong bobbies and together, we'll go to Manor House to arrest Bumpkin. He is either dead, or wounded severely enough to not put up much resistance. Personally, I even wonder if he had enough life in him to climb over that wall."

We did just that. We woke up the landlord at the Trusted Servant, who was thrilled to meet the famous Sherlock Holmes; in fact he was so happy that he made no objection to my having "borrowed" Toby to help me in the hunt for the Lyndhurst killer.

While Holmes was enjoying a bowl of hot chicken broth, the landlord's teenage son rode on his bike to Lyndhurst with a note from Holmes to Constable Goodfield, requesting the assistance of two men.

A couple of hours later, not just the two bobbies but also Goodfield in person showed up at the pub. I guessed that the Constable didn't want to risk letting go of any of the credit attached to the capture of the killer.

A few minutes later, I rang at the gate of the Lunatic Asylum. It was about 10 a.m. and it looked as if it was going to be a hot day.

The same orderly answered and, if he was intimidated by the sight of five men, three of whom were in uniform, he showed no signs of it.

"We want to talk to Dr. Smythe," I said.

"Yes, sir. He is very busy right now, but I will announce you. If you'd like to follow me to the waiting room?"

"Thank you," I said, "but I think we'll wait outside."

We sat on a stone bench in front of the director's office, while the orderly disappeared under the arcades surrounding the body of the main building. To the right I could see the new edifice that had been built thanks to Lord Beltham's largesse.

"I bet Bumpkin went missing last night," I said to Holmes. "That is why Smythe isn't so eager to see us!

He must have expected our visit. Ultimately, the responsibility for what happened will be his. I'm sure he's not looking forward to it."

Orderlies came and went, moving equipment from the old to the new building, looking concerned or confused by the presence of three policemen in their midst.

A quarter of an hour later, Dr. Smythe finally appeared.

"I'm so sorry to have kept you waiting, gentlemen," he said, displaying no signs of anxiety at all, which I thought a little odd. "We're having the ceremony for the inauguration of our new wing this afternoon, and there's a myriad of small details that need to be taken care of. I know why you're here..."

I had been informally elected to be the spokesman for our group, so I answered:

"You do?"

"Yes, of course. Follow me. He's at the infirmary."

As we walked, Smythe continued:

"Who could have predicted something like that? No, don't tell me... You saw how much kindness I bestow upon all my patients, Mr. Dickson... But with just a moment's carelessness, something bad happens... Ah! My God! What a tragedy! And the day before our new wing is to be opened! It couldn't have been worse!"

"There's probably not much you could have done," I said, trying to interrupt his verbal diarrhea.

"You are too good, sir," said the unfortunate director, "but I will never forgive myself for what happened. If only we could do something for that unfortunate soul, but no, he's barely breathing... beyond any medical help... He'll expire at any minute now."

"We still want to see him," I said.

"But certainly, Mr. Dickson, though it's not a very pretty sight, I assure you..."

We climbed a small stone staircase and arrived in front of a building facade, on which we read the word etched into the rock: *Infirmary*.

Dr. Smythe pushed a glass door and we found ourselves in a small rectangular room filled with the sickening smell of carbolic and water poultice.

Four white percale curtains-adorned beds occupied the four corners of the room, and in front of one of these stood a gentleman in a black coat.

He was the doctor.

On hearing us enter, he turned abruptly and made a desperate sign to Dr. Smythe.

I walked to the bed and could not suppress a cry of surprise.

The man lying there, with his bluish face and bloodshot eyes, was not Bumpkin!

He was a poor, little, sickly individual, whose head was hardly bigger than two fists.

"What's the meaning of this?" I cried. "Who is this man? Where is Bumpkin?"

"Bumpkin?" said Dr. Smythe. "I thought you knew what had happened... that someone had told you about poor Bischoff trying to kill himself."

"I'm not interested in Bischoff," I cried. "It's Bumpkin I want to see. Where is he?"

"In his cell, of course. Where else?" replied the director with a genuine air of surprise.

"Are you certain?"

"Yes."

"I'm not! I want to see Bumpkin in his cell—and check that he's OK."

For once, Dr. Smythe seemed confused.

"I don't understand. Why wouldn't he be OK?"

"Take me to this cell," I ordered.

The hapless director shrugged, then led us through various sections of the asylum, until we finally reached the wing allocated for the patients prone to violence.

At a quick glance, I saw all the lunatics whom I had seen the day before.

Bumpkin was not among them.

"So where is he?" I said.

Smythe approached Tripp, who, surprised by our unexpected visit, had been trying to hide under his jacket a huge cherrywood baton that he must have been using to keep his wards in line, despite the regulations—but I didn't care.

"Mr. Tripp, where is inmate Bumpkin?" roared Smythe.

Tripp replied in a thick voice:

"He's been agitated since yesterday; I had to leave him in the shed."

"You lie," I yelled. "He's escaped."

The orderly dropped his baton. He looked confused. He was prone to drinking and his memory occasionally failed him. He thought he had locked up Bumpkin the night before, but was he still there? The only thing was to make sure.

He walked to a shed at the end of the courtyard. We heard the noise of latches being drawn, keys being jingled, lock being unlocked, a creaking door being pushed open loudly, then he reappeared, dragging behind him the dreaded Bumpkin who was shouting beastly howls.

He also appeared to be totally unharmed—with not a single bullet wound on him!

This time, Dr. Smythe looked at me sternly and I guessed that he thought I might well join his cohorts.

"As you see," he said, "Bumpkin has not escaped. No one has ever escaped from this facility, gentlemen."

I approached the lunatic and examined him carefully, trying to spot any bloodstains or at least the tears that might have been produced by the bullets of my Browning.

Nothing! Bumpkin's clothes were intact.

Was I going mad? How could I be so wrong?

I insisted that we undress the madman, and Dr. Smythe agreed, if only to stop my grumbling.

Bumpkin's body showed no injury.

The man whom I had shot had been hit; I was sure of it, since I had found traces of blood on the ground. Therefore, that man was not Bumpkin.

What happened to me then, I can barely relate here. I was so utterly bewildered that I might have yielded to god knows what terrible impulses if Sherlock Holmes had not stepped in and said, in a calm voice:

"Why don't we go back to the place where the attack took place and retrace the path the monster took. It is obvious that he didn't come here."

"Toby!" I cried.

"What?"

"Toby will be able to follow the trail! Why didn't I think of this before?"

Hurriedly, we left Manor House after apologizing profusely to Dr. Smythe.

Half an hour later, we were back at the spot where my mentor had almost succumbed to the Monster's assault.

I held Toby on a long lead, which had been supplied by his master.

Before us were only broken branches, a gutted coppice, and I noticed wide tracks that seemed to have been produced by a hulkish man.

On the grass, I saw a blood stain, then a bit further, I found another.

"I knew I had hit him!" I cried. "This confirms it!"

Widespread red drops everywhere indicated the path followed by the monster.

I thought we might find him dead in a thicket.

"Seek, my good boy! Seek!" I ordered Toby.

The dog started off like a rocket and it was difficult for us—especially, Holmes—to follow him through the woods and brambles, but we managed to stay abreast of him.

At some point, a larger bloody mark got our attention.

"Here," said Holmes. "See how the grass is trampled around this pool of blood... Our wounded man certainly fell here... then he got up and left that way."

In a thicket we could see a kind of hole that extended to a small trail cutting through the woods in the direction of what was obviously our destination.

I couldn't repress a gasp of surprise.

It was the priory of Reverend Patterson!

CHAPTER XXI
The Reverend's Last Revelation and What Ensued

For nearly three-quarters of an hour, we had followed the trail of the assassin breathlessly—literally—and now, as we were about to come face to face with the dreaded and elusive Lyndhurst Murderer, we seemed disarmed.

"The Reverend? Could it be...?" whispered Goodfield with a sigh that might have been either from shock or relief.

We stood there, looking at the darkened house, listening attentively, trying to catch some moaning, some complaint, coming from that frightening abyss.

But no noise, no light, rose from the Priory.

"Let's go in," I whispered.

I tied Toby to a pole outside, then, as silently as I could, I turned the door handle and, one after the other, we stepped inside.'

Suddenly, Holmes, who had keen vision, thought he distinguished something gray and bulky, about ten feet away on the floor.

"Do you see that?" he said, pointing at the thing.

"Yes," I replied. "It must be the Reverend."

As the shape didn't move, Goodfield instructed one of his men to turn on the lights.

My mentor had been correct: it was indeed the form of Reverend Patterson, wrapped inside a gray fur automobilist coat, who lay on the floor.

I could see at once that he was still alive, although barely, as I detected a faint breath coming out of his mouth. No doubt his bulky coat had cushioned the blow of my bullets, but I realized he wasn't long for this world.

I kneeled by his side to talk to him.

"Reverend," I said, "talk to us, tell us the truth. Were you the Lyndhurst Murderer?"

"Yes," he whispered in a ragged, raspy voice. "It was I... all along..."

"We have our man," said Goodfield, with a satisfied smug. "Congratulations to the two of you. Job well done!"

But just then, the dying man whispered:

"Carl... will be safe... now."

Having uttered that last sentence, he died.

Out of habit more than hoping to achieve something in particular, I felt the dead man's pockets and pulled out a small gray wallet, soiled by use.

I opened it and pulled out a letter and an old photograph of a very beautiful woman. On the back of it were the initials "E.P."

The letter was written in French; it was an affidavit of birth that read:

"I, the undersigned, Pierre Michel, do hereby state and attest that the following is true and accurate to the best of my knowledge: On this day, the 22nd of June, 1867, was born twin boys, Carl and Pierre, to Joseph Fipart and Ellen Palmure, and I know of their births because of my relationship with their father. I hereby attest to the fact that birth records for these two individuals were impossible to obtain and that a birth certificate was not issued upon their births.

Signed: Pierre Michel, Mayor of Kerloven, Brittany."

"That must be a photograph of Ellen Palmure," I said. "She was very beautiful."

"One of the men working for her father was named Patterson," said Holmes. "I never made the connection. Of course, it is a very common name..."

"So Patterson was the one who took Carl back to England... The future Fantômas."

"Yes, so it would seem," said my mentor.

"He said that he grew up nearby..." I whispered to myself. "Yes, that would explain it!"

"Have you found something, Harry?" asked Holmes.

"Yes! I think I solved the case!" Then, after a pause, I added:

"By Jove! What a diabolical plan!"

Goodfield now seemed more confused than ever.

"What do we do now, Mr. Holmes?" he asked my mentor.

"We follow Harry Dickson!" answered my friend with a smile.

"We must hurry," I said. "I only pray that we'll be in time to stop the one murder that has always been the only thing that mattered to our invisible enemy."

"And what murder is that?"asked Goodfield.

"Why, that of Lord Beltham, of course!"

The following was excerpted from the Deposition of Lord William Beltham taken by Constable Goodfield the following day, June 15th, 1910. It was found attached in the journals of Harry Dickson at that point in the narrative:

When I arrived at Manor House, I found with some pleasure that cold cuts and refreshments had been provided by the staff under a tent set up in the main court-yard.

After exchanging some pleasantries with Dr. Smythe, and discussing the arrangements for his impending marriage to my daughter, Alice, he offered to show me the new wing.

We embarked upon the visit, just he and I, and everything was perfectly normal until we walked down to an underground level where, according to him, cells had been built to accommodate "special cases."

There were indeed four such cells, heavily padded, with one-way sliding doors in the back connecting, I assumed, to the rest of the asylum. The front wall of each cell had a large one-way glass partition—"totally unbreakable," Smythe assured me—that enabled the medical staff to monitor the patients around the clock without being seen themselves.

Smythe wished me to see how the glass would look from inside the cells—I had assumed it would be a mirror, but it turned out to be a flat, grey panel—and unwarily, I stepped inside.

I felt a chill run down my spine when I heard the characteristic sound of the door being bolted me behind me.

If I couldn't see Smythe, there must have been a hidden microphone embedded in the walls, for I heard his voice very clearly—except it was no longer his voice, the voice of the Smythe I knew, but that of another man, whom I thought had died long ago.

"You're my prisoner now, William," the voice said. "But rest assured, you won't be for long. I only need a couple of minutes to set up things on my side to prove later that I did my utmost to get you out of there, and that the tragic fate that's going to befall you was only a horrible accident."

"*Carl?*" I uttered, not wanting to be right, yet knowing from the tightness in my chest that I wasn't wrong.

"You recognized my voice right away! Very good!" he chuckled. "Well, it seems this is a day for old acquaintances to be reunited. Guess who is behind that door which I'm going to open in a few seconds?"

"Why are you doing this, Carl? Let me go. I never did anything to you. I was always good to you! It was Edward who... who... did things to you..."

"I hate you!" he spat with such fury that I involuntarily took a step back. "I hated all of you! And after you're gone, and I've married your sow of a daughter, and seized your fortune, trust me, I look forward to the day not far distant when I'll become a widower, ah! ah!"

"No! Not Alice!" I screamed. "Kill me if you must! It's true! I did nothing to help you... I could have... But Alice is innocent! Let her be! Please, Carl, divorce her, but don't kill her! Please!"

"Come now, William! Where would be the fun in that? And don't call me Carl anymore. I buried that name long ago. In fact, it died under the executioner's blade in Paris. Today, my name is..."

"What?"

"...*Fantômas!*"

I fell to my knees, knowing that all hope had gone, and entrusting my soul to the Lord.

The door to the back of the cell began to slide upward.

As I heard that furious roar, I knew who stood behind it, and that my death would be neither quick, nor painless.

"Bom-Ko," I stammered, as I beheld the ferocious man-ape, shaven, but unable to hide his bestial origins.

"Bel-tam!" screamed the beast in fury, before stepping inside the cell.

Of course, I knew who he was. My brother had confessed our family's darkest secret to me long ago.

I closed my eyes, preparing to die under the fangs and claws of the man-ape.

Suddenly, I heard three gunshots, followed by a fall that made the floor shake.

I opened my eyes: a man stood on the threshold of the sliding door, a smoking revolver still in his right hand.

It was Harry Dickson!

CHAPTER XXII
The Truth at last!

We never caught Fantômas.

By the time the police invaded the new wing's underground level, he had vanished. Later, they found a secret tunnel leading to a cave deep inside the New Forest, with signs of a car having been parked there. The bird had flown the coop.

We returned to Minstead, then Lyndhurst, where Goodfield reassured the population and the press that they had nothing more to fear from the mysterious madman who had terrorized the region.

It is hardly necessary to consign in these pages the triumphal reception that was given to us when they heard that the great Sherlock Holmes and his "clever assistant" (that is what they called me) had finally brought peace to the country again.

Women were especially thrilled, because many used to go at nightfall to take the air near the woods, and had given up this habit while the monster was at large—and their husbands had complained loudly that their wives had been in foul moods since.

For me, it was the first time that I had met such a triumph in England, and it set my future career on the path that I would follow.

Toby was held in special esteem and people came from everywhere to see the dog who had helped capture the new Jack the Ripper.

A young lady offered me her hand with several thousands of pounds in dowry, but I declined the offer on the advice of my mentor who claimed that I could "do better."

We could have stayed in Southampton for a few more days, which would not have displeased me, but Holmes felt the need to return to Baker Street.

"London's calling us, Harry!" he said to me. "Come! We have to work to do!"

The next day, with the two of us comfortably settled in deep, leather armchairs, Mrs. Hudson having brewed us a delicious cup of tea, I recapped the matter for the benefit of my mentor:

"This is what I think happened," I said by way of introduction. "Rocambole and Ellen Palmure had twin sons, Carl and Paul. Carl was taken to Lyndhurst by Ellen's former henchman, Patterson, who was as devoted to him as if he'd been his own son, but eventually entrusted him to the Belthams to give him a better start in life.

"Young Carl fell under Edward Beltham—Lord Beltham's—evil influence. According to Edward's brother, William, the boy was abused. You know what evil fruits may spring from those seeds...

"Later, as you yourself told me, you found out that Lord Beltham was financing mad Doctor Moreau's abominable research. The *Matilda Briggs*, which belonged to his family's shipping empire, was used to supply Moreau's island and, in return, she brought several of Moreau's experiments, including a simian hybrid named Bom-Ko, back to London to be used in Edward's monstrous orgies.

"Bom-Ko, wanting to be more human, escaped and committed the 'Jack the Ripper' murders, believing that, by absorbing his victims' life essence, he could somehow evolve. I'm not sure all the blame here should belong to Moreau. I did some research and there was an account published five years ago by a Frenchman named Jules Lermina drawn from reports by Dutch colonists, which mentions a tribe of evolved man-apes led by one named To-Ho... Still, I suppose Moreau carried this secret with him to his grave...

"After you exposed the scandal, Edward Beltham was spared because of his royal connections, but forced to leave England; the *Matilda Briggs* and her crew are allowed to go free in exchange for their silence; and Moreau's island was blown up by the British Navy. Bom-Ko was thought to have been euthanized, but in reality, he was kept prisoner at an asylum run by a Dr. Lionel Prospero McDuff, who may or may not have been Moreau himself—if he had managed to escape his island's destruction. We'll never learn that truth of that.

"I found some of Doctor McDuff's papers at the Asylum, which Smythe had not destroyed. Apparently, he was looking for a cure for spinal meningitis, and had injected Bom-Ko with a serum of his own invention, which he called 'Virus 669,' that had the unfortunate side effect of turning him into a savage, homicidal maniac.

"Five years later, Lord Beltham terrorized Berlin by committing a series of bloody murders, and there, he coined the alias of 'Fantômas.' Unsurprisingly, he was helped in his crime spree by none other than Carl, but the two split soon after. Carl went on to become an international bandit in the U.S., Mexico, and finally in South Africa where, during the Boer War, he met again with his evil mentor.

"But this time, something was different: Carl fell in love with Lord Beltham's new wife, Maud. In 1900, they returned to Europe, Beltham caught Carl in bed with Maud, and Carl strangled him. Exit Edward, and his younger brother, William, now became the new Lord Beltham.

"Carl took over the convenient alias of Fantômas and went on his own murder spree. Meanwhile, in Malaysia, Bom-Ko's partner, Sho-Po, finally located the *Matilda Briggs*. Disguised as a sailor named 'Bill Sharper,' he embarked on the ship to look for Bom-Ko. Were these two brothers? Friends? Lovers even? Frankly, I doubt we'll ever find out. But they were certainly greatly attached to each other.

"In June 1906, the *Matilda Briggs* stopped in London. Somehow, Sho-Po managed to locate Dr. McDuff's asylum and forced him to release Bom-Ko. However, on June 13, he killed a school mistress. So Sho-Po had to take him back to the Asylum. To be safe, McDuff decided to move to Portsmouth, but it was too late. Fantômas had become alerted to the possibility that Bom-Ko may still be alive."

"So did I," said Holmes. "But all the trails led nowhere."

"Indeed. The following year, again in June, the *Matilda Briggs* stopped in Portsmouth. The same thing happened: Sho-Po saw Bom-Ko, but another murder followed. This time, McDuff decided to move his establishment to Scotland.

"In December 1908, the *Matilda Briggs* stopped in Glasgow; this time, Bom-Ko killed a young Irishwoman before the ship left. But Fantômas had found enough clues to locate McDuff. He killed him, and, disguised as Doctor Smythe, took over the asylum, which he moved to Lyndhurst. Once there, he caused William Beltham to hire the Johnson Brothers and renewed his acquaintance with Patterson. Finally, he began courting Alice, William's daughter, his ultimate goal being to marry her, kill William and grab the Belthams' fortune.

"A year ago in March, the *Matilda Briggs* stopped in Dover. The Johnson Brothers took Bom-Ko to meet Sho-Po; once again, the monster killed, this time two prostitutes. Through the brothers, Fantômas expressed his desire to meet Sho-Po the next time he was in England."

"By then, I had begun to see the pattern," said Holmes, "the connection between the murders and the stopovers of the *Matilda Briggs*, but the overall picture was still too vague. There was nothing pointing to either the Belthams or Fantômas."

"In May of this year, through an exchange of correspondence, Fantômas arranged to meet Sho-Po the following month at the Johnsons' house. On June 3, the ship arrived in Southampton with Sho-Po—Bill Sharper—aboard. On the night of June 5, Fantômas released Bom-Ko, who killed Betty Beaton in Lyndhurst. Sho-Po arrived too late to save the poor woman.

"On the night of June 7, Fantômas finally met Sho-Po at the Johnsons' house. The conversation went badly and Fantômas killed him. We'll never find out what went wrong, but I suppose Fantômas wanted Sho-Po to kill William in exchange for releasing Bom-Ko and Sho-Po turned him down.

"Two days later, the Johnson Brothers were arrested and we found Sho-Po's body. Fantômas now had no choice: he had to use Bom-Ko to kill William, but being the unreliable, out-of-control creature he was, he escaped and killed another woman, just by Manor House in Minstead.

"Meanwhile, Patterson had figured out Fantômas's plan. He had loved Carl; if he knew that Lord Beltham had abused his ward, he must have felt guilty for placing him there. In order to protect Carl and help him achieve his goals, he decided to pretend to be the killer himself, and attacked the first person he saw walking alone at night, whom, as we know, was you, in the guise of Mr. Charcott.

"We could have been fooled, but the links we found between Patterson and Carl in the dead man's wallet, and the connection between Smythe and Lyndhurst which he had unwittingly revealed to me the day before, clicked in my mind, and I suddenly grasped the entirety of Fantômas' devilish plan!"

"That was very well deduced, Harry! Now you need to write it down, since you have no amanuensis to record your cases."

"Dr. Watson is one in a million, Mr. Holmes. You've been very lucky there. I doubt I'll ever find his like."

Afterword

What are the major differences between the original *L'Homme au Complet Gris* and *The Man in Grey*?

As explained in our introduction, we have merged Allan Dickson into the better known Harry Dickson, but that required no changes other than switching their respective Christian names.

Holmes (Herlokolms in the original) required more work, since Galopin's characterization of the Great Detective was very poor. Principally, we threw out a pointless, unmotivated fight, full of bitterness and professional jealousy, between Holmes and Dickson in Chapter XV, entirely uncharacteristic of either character, and serving no purpose, plot-wise.

As is the case with all of our retold adaptations, we smoothed out the narrative and, especially, patched up a few glaring plot holes and inconsistencies left by Galopin, usually by providing our own explanations for what was left unsaid.

For instance, the two ape-men (Bill Sharper and Bumpkin) played the same respective parts in the original novel, but their origins, as well as the connection between them, was left unexplained. Galopin probably borrowed the notion of a murderous man-ape from Edgar Poe's famous *Murders in the Rue Morgue*, but felt no need to elucidate, or simply ran out of steam.

The link between the murders in the novel and the historical Jack the Ripper crimes, much teased in the early part of the book, eventually leads to no revelations whatsoever. Was the original Jack a man-ape as well? The same man-ape? And if so, how? The book remains confused on this subject.

Hence, enter H.G. Wells' Dr. Moreau in our adaptation, as well as a tighter connection to the original Ripper crimes via the history of the Belthams, which in turn brought in the character of Fantômas. The connection with Rocambole and Jules Lermina's novel *To-Ho and the Gold Destroyers*, also dealing with remarkably evolved man-apes, are just bonuses, entirely made up by the undersigned, with zero impact on the plot. Ellen Palmure in *Rocambole* did have a henchman disguised as a Reverend that went by the name of Peter Town, close enough to Patterson to merge the two.

Mind you, in the original novel, the puppet master is indeed Dr. Smythe (actually named "Dr. Sly"), so except for making him an alias of Fantômas, we didn't change that, except that his part was split between two characters, the other Doctor, nominally in charge of the Asylum, being called "Dr. Ovid Chatterbox!"

And of course, in Galopin's novel, "Dr. Sly/Smythe" is not seeking to marry Alice in order to grab the Beltham fortune. In fact, after reading the book, we're left wondering what it was exactly that Sly/Smythe hoped to gain by unleashing a murderous man-ape upon the British countryside. The ending of the original novel is rushed and, frankly, a bit of a mess.

The part played by the younger Beltham in our adaptation is attributed to a local industrialist named "Mr. Strumpf." In fact, Galopin had a pretty bad ear for English names, so out went "Strumpf," "Bigrump," "Plentiful," "Crasscott," etc., to be replaced by more authentic-sounding names. The ship that carried Bill Sharper (his name remains unchanged) was called the *Arabella* in the original, and not the *Matilda Briggs*, of course, but the temptation to add a further link to the Holmesian canon was too great to be ignored.

The last two chapters are mostly our own; in Galopin's version, the man-ape falls in a convenient sink hole in the woods and the mad Doctor Sly explains he'd been injected with an experimental virus of his own invention (Virus 669) intended to cure spinal meningitis, which turned him savage, and he escaped and killed the two women.

One is left with the notion that the whole thing was just a horrible experiment gone wrong, relegating the entire "Jack the Ripper" angle, which had been so important earlier in the book, to total irrelevancy.

All in all, there is no doubt in our mind that, had Arnould Galopin devoted more time to *L'Homme au Complet Gris*, he likely would have provided his own fixes to the problems mentioned above. Those would certainly have not involved Dr. Moreau or Fantômas, but they would have been likely derivative from the same archetypes of a mad scientist and a criminal mastermind. Our retelling may be more fanciful, but it is not substantially different from the original.

Jean-Marc & Randy Lofficier

Timeline

This retold version of *The Man in Grey* draws on the respective chronologies of Sherlock Holmes, Harry Dickson, Fantômas, Arsène Lupin, H. G. Wells' *The Island of Doctor Moreau* and Jules Lermina's *To-Ho and the Gold Destroyers*, and also, to a lesser degree, those of Rocambole and Tarzan.

We have prepared the following timeline in order to enlighten the readers who enjoy this kind of literary exercise. Needless to say, none of what follows is necessary for the enjoyment of the novel, which overall remains extremely faithful to Galopin's original plot.

1854.
Birth of Sherlock Holmes to Siger Holmes and Violet Sherrinford.

1858.
Birth of Edward Beltham of Scottwell Hill. The Belthams are connected to the Royal Family.

1866.
Birth of William Beltham, Edward's younger brother.

1867.
Birth of Carl (the future Fantômas) and Paul (the future Juve) in Brittany to Rocambole and Ellen Palmure. Rocambole perished fighting the Germans c. 1870; Ellen's fate is unknown.

1868.
Paul is raised by Anne-Marie Juve, the midwife. Carl is taken to the village of Lyndhurst in Sussex to be raised by Ellen Palmure's former henchman, Patterson, now Reverend Patterson.

1874.
Patterson entrusts a seven-year-old Carl to the Belthams; the youth progressively falls under Edward's malefic influence.

1881.
July. Sherlock Holmes meets Dr. John H. Watson and takes up residence in Baker Street (*A Study in Scarlet*).

1882.
Birth of Maud Greystoke. The Greystokes are connected to the Royal Family.

1885.
Edward, now Lord Beltham, finances Dr. Moreau's research. The *Matilda Briggs*, which belongs to the Belthams, supplies Moreau's island.
An eighteen-year-old Carl travels to India as the Belthams' agent and claims Rocambole's inheritance. (*Fantômas 32: The Death of Fantômas*)

1887.
The *Matilda Briggs* brings several of Dr. Moreau's experiments to London for Edward's orgies, including a simian hybrid named Bom-Ko.

1888.

February. Birth of Harry Allan Dickson in New York to Edgar Arthur Dickson, a stage magician, and an Australian woman whom he met while touring in Sydney.

August-November. The mentally disturbed Bom-Ko escapes and, wanting to be "more human" by absorbing other women's life-force, commits the "Jack the Ripper" murders:

August 7: Martha Tabram.

August 31: Polly Nichols.

September 8: Annie Chapman.

September 30: Elizabeth Stride and Catharine Eddowes.

November 9: Mary Jane Kelly.

November. Sherlock Holmes secretly solves the Ripper murders.

December. As a result, Lord Beltham is exiled from England; the scandal is suppressed because of his royal family connection. The *Matilda Briggs* and her crew are allowed to go free.

1889.

February. The island of Dr. Moreau is destroyed by the British Navy on Mycroft's orders.

March. Pendrick, a survivor from the destruction of Dr. Moreau's island, is picked up by British Navy. (*The Island of Dr. Moreau* - story not told by H.G. Wells until 1896.)

Dr. Moreau also escapes and returns to England under the guise of "Dr. Lionel P. McDuff," under which he operates a private asylum in London.

Bom-Ko is believed to have been killed but is, in fact, still prisoner at Dr. McDuff's asylum for research purposes (trying to cure spinal meningitis).

1891.

Spring. Carl, now calling himself "Archduke Juan North," operates in the German Principality of Heisse-Weimar. (*Fantômas 5: Un Roi Prisonnier de Fantômas/A Royal Prisoner*)

June. Birth of Alice, daughter of William Beltham, at Scottwell Hill.

1892.

January. Carl/Juan North has a son, Vladimir, with the aunt of future king Frederick-Christian. (*Fantômas 5: Un Roi Prisonnier de Fantômas/A Royal Prisoner*)

March. Juan North is arrested and sent to prison. (*Fantômas 5: Un Roi Prisonnier de Fantômas/A Royal Prisoner*)

April. Sherlock Holmes duels with Professor Moriarty at the Reichenbach Falls. (*The Final Problem*)

1893.

January. The Dicksons are in Paris. Edgar trains a young Arsène Lupin.

March-December. Lord Beltham (now a serial killer) terrorizes Berlin with Juan's help coining the alias of "Fantômas." (*The Fantômas of Berlin*)

1894.

April. Sherlock Holmes returns to London. (*The Empty House*)

Events of *To-Ho and the Gold Destroyers* (Part 1).

1895.

February. Birth of Charles Rambert (the future Jérôme Fandor) (*Fantômas 27: Le Cadavre Géant*)

March. Birth of the grand-daughter of the last king of India, Bedjapur; to save her life, his followers take the baby to South Africa. (*Fantômas 32: The Death of Fantômas*)

1896.
Harry Dickson is sent to various public schools in England. During the summer, he returns to New York.

1897.
January. Now in New York, Juan North meets, then partners with, businessman Etienne Rambert.
March. Juan North ruins Rambert and flees to Mexico. (*Fantômas 29: La Série Rouge*)

1898.
February. Juan North embarks for South Africa and joins the Boers under the name of "Gurn." (*Fantômas 8: The Daughter of Fantômas*)
April. Gurn partners with Hans Helder to set up a diamond trafficking ring. (*Fantômas 8: The Daughter of Fantômas*)
June. In Paris, Lord Beltham marries Maud Greystoke, hoping to use her own family connections to be allowed to return to England.
November. Birth of Hélène, from Gurn and an unknown mother.

1899.
October. The Boer War starts. Gurn betrays the Boers, joins the British Army, and becomes an artillery sergeant under the command of Lord Roberts; he uses the war to enrich himself. (*Fantômas 8: The Daughter of Fantômas*)

November. Lord Beltham arrives in South Africa. He and Gurn renew their acquaintance. Gurn meets Maud. (*Fantômas 1*)

1900.

May. Gurn leaves South Africa to return to England with the Belthams. His affair with Maud begins on the ship taking them back to England. (*Fantômas 1*)

July. Beltham surprises Gurn and his wife in bed in his apartment in Paris. Gurn strangles him and assumes the mantle of Fantômas. (*Fantômas 1*)

December. The new Fantômas kills the Marquise de Langrune. (*Fantômas 1*)

1901.

June. Fantômas robs Princess Sonia Danidoff. (*Fantômas 1*)

August. Juve arrests Fantômas who is condemned to death. (*Fantômas 1*) (Juve doesn't realize that Fantômas is his brother.)

1902.

January. Fantômas escapes the guillotine by substituting an actor in his place. (*Fantômas 1*)

February. Fantômas blows up the Belthams' Parisian residence. He and Maud leave France. (*Fantômas 2: Juve contre Fantômas/The Exploits of Juve*)

July. Arsène Lupin burglarizes Thibermesnil Castle and crosses swords with Sherlock Holmes for the first time. (*Sherlock Holmes Arrives Too Late*)

1903.

June. Harry Dickson wins a Junior Boxing Championship in Queens.

December. Sherlock Holmes retires to Sussex.

Using the alias of "Paul Daubreuil," Arsène Lupin saves Jeanne Darcieux from her stepfather's diabolical scheme. (*La Mort Qui Rôde*)

He also steals Professor Gerbois' valuable desk (*The Blonde Phantom*)

1904.

February. Arsène Lupin and a mysterious female accomplice, the so-called "Blonde Phantom," deal with the matter of the winning lottery ticket found in Professor Gerbois' stolen desk. (*The Blonde Phantom*)

March. The Blonde Phantom is accused of the murder of Baron d'Hautrec. (*The Blonde Phantom*)

April. Fantômas, back in France, murders Jacques Dollon in order to steal his identity. (*Fantômas 3: Le Mort qui tue/Messengers of Evil*)

May. Fantômas becomes involved in espionage. (*Fantômas 4: L'Agent Secret/A Nest of Spies*)

June. Maud Beltham finds refuge in Heisse-Weimar.

July. Jeanne Darcieux marries Lord Strongborough (*Arsène Lupin Arrives too Late*)

August-September. The case of the murder of Baron d'Hautrec resurfaces: the Baron's Blue Diamond is stolen at the chateau de Crozon. Ganimard investigates fruitlessly; Sherlock Holmes is finally summoned to find the Blue Diamond. (*The Blonde Phantom*)

September. A fifteen-year-old Harry Dickson solves the Blessington Problem while attending the Pertwee Private School in England (*Le Problème Blessington*); he attracts Holmes' attention; they begin a correspondence. He also meets armchair detective Mr. Triggs.

October. Sherlock Holmes and Watson, have a chance meeting with Arsène Lupin and Leblanc in a Paris restaurant. Holmes eventually discovers Lupin's use of secret passages in houses he designed as "Maxime Bermont." Holmes delivers Lupin into the hands of Ganimard, but the Gentleman Burglar makes a daring escape and is at the station to say good-bye to the Great Detective. (*The Blonde Phantom*)

November. Arsène Lupin leaves France and travels successively to Uruguay, Antarctica and Saigon. Murder of Lord Strongborough (*Arsène Lupin Arrives Too Late*)

December. Lady Strongborough is arrested. (*Arsène Lupin Arrives Too Late*)

Fantômas kidnaps the King of Heisse-Weimar. (*Fantômas 5: Un Roi Prisonnier de Fantômas/A Royal Prisoner*)

Events of *To-Ho and the Gold Destroyers* (Part 2).

1905.

January. Journalist Jérôme Fandor (Etienne Rambert's son) frees the King of Heisse-Weimar. Mistaken for Fantômas, Juve is arrested. (*Fantômas 5: Un Roi Prisonnier de Fantômas/A Royal Prisoner*)

March. Arsène Lupin is in Armenia and in Turkey, where he fights the Red Sultan. (*Arsène Lupin Arrives too Late*)

April. Lady Strongborough is sentenced to death. Delayed by his battle with the Red Sultan, Lupin arrives in Marseilles. (*Arsène Lupin Arrives too Late*)

May. Fantômas impersonates the American detective Tom Bob. (*Fantômas 6: Le Policier Apache/The Long Arm of Fantômas*)

June. Arsène Lupin meets with Lady Strongborough in Saint Paul de Vence. (*Arsène Lupin Arrives too Late*)

July. Juve is freed. Fantômas escapes to England. *(Fantômas 6: Le Policier Apache/The Long Arm of Fantômas)*

September. In Malaysia, Bom-Ko's mate, Sho-Po, finally locates the *Matilda Briggs*; disguised as a sailor named "Bill Sharper," he embarks upon the ship to look for Bom-Ko.

1906.

February. While in London, Fantômas operates under the aliases of Tom Bob, Dr. Garrick and Sâr Hamashkim. He clashes with Sherlock Holmes, assisted by Harry Dickson who is doing some odd jobs for Nick Carter. (*Sherlock Holmes vs. Fantômas*)

June. The *Matilda Briggs* stops in London. Sho-Po manages to locate Dr. Moreau/McDuff, and forces him to release Bom-Ko. On June 13, he kills a school mistress from Hammersmith. Sho-Po takes him back to Moreau's asylum. Moreau moves to Portsmouth.

As a result of this crime, Both Holmes and Fantômas become aware that Bom-Ko may still be alive.

1907.

April. Second encounter between Sherlock Holmes and Fantômas. (*The Grand Horizontals*)

Fantômas plots to blackmail Lord Ascott. (*Fantômas 7: Le Pendu de Londres*)

June. At Sho-Po's urging, the *Matilda Briggs* stops in Portsmouth. Sho-Po sees Bom-Ko again, but he commits another murder. Moreau is forced to move to Scotland.

September. Edgar Dickson and his wife retire to Western Australia where they become farmers. Soon after, Edgar is murdered. Harry swears to avenge him and captures

219

his killers. He decides to become a professional detective.

1908.

January-March. Harry Dickson solves his first cases: *The Devil's Hand, The Murders of the Broadway Hotel The Affair of Grosvenor House, The Orange-Colored Room.*

April. Fantômas kidnaps Fandor and ships him to South Africa. (*Fantômas 7: Le Pendu de Londres/Slippery as Sin*)

May. Fantômas is arrested by Scotland Yard. (*Fantômas 7: Le Pendu de Londres/Slippery as Sin*)

June. Fantômas is condemned to hang but, with Juve's help, fakes his death. (*Fantômas 8: The Daughter of Fantômas*)

Arsène Lupin challenges Holmes again in the case of the Imblevalle Robbery. Holmes lets go of Lupin on the *Ville-de-Londres*. Lupin advises Alice Demun to contact Lady Strongborough. (*The Jewish Lamp*)

July. Fantômas travels to South Africa. Juve follows. Fandor meets Hand falls in love with Hélène. (*Fantômas 8: The Daughter of Fantômas*)

July-December. In London, Arsène Lupin (unbeknownst to Holmes at first) teams up with Irene Adler to fight Professor Flax in the Case of the Silver Knight. Lupin escapes one of Holmes' traps, but is later recognized by Watson (*The Unkindest Cut*)

August. Harry Dickson meets and falls in love with Irène de Hautefeuille. (*Le Rituel de la Mort*)

December. Back in Paris, Fantômas renews his affair with Maud. (*Fantômas 9: Le Fiacre de Nuit*)

The *Matilda Briggs* stops in Glasgow; this time, Bom-Ko kills a young Irishwoman. Fantômas finds Dr. Moreau, kills him, takes over the asylum under the disguise of "Dr. Smythe," and moves it to Lyndhurst. There he causes William Beltham to hire the Johnson Brothers and renews his acquaintance with Patterson. Finally, he begins courting Alice, William Beltham's daughter.

1909.

January. March. Harry Dickson solves the mysterious Affair of Green Park. (*La Ténébreuse Affaire de Green Park*)

February. Fantômas loots the casino of Monte-Carlo. (*Fantômas 10: La Main Coupée/The Limb of Satan*)

March. The *Matilda Briggs* stops in Dover. The Johnson Brothers take Bom-Ko to meet Sho-Po; he kills two young prostitutes. Fantômas expresses his desire to meet Sho-Po next time the *Matilda Briggs* stops in England.

April. Fantômas is arrested in Belgium. (*Fantômas 11: L'Arrestation de Fantômas*)

April-June. Arsène Lupin's latest round of burglaries catches the attention of Isidore Beautrelet, who becomes fascinated by the mystery of the Hollow Needle. Soon, Lupin faces not only Beautrelet and Ganimard, but also Sherlock Holmes. Lupin falls in love with the beautiful Raymonde de Saint-Veran, initially believed to be his victim. (*The Hollow Needle*)

June-October. Arsène Lupin has Holmes and Ganimard kidnapped. He fakes his own death and that of Raymonde. As "Louis Valmeras," he marries Raymonde in October, then decides to go straight and live a peaceful life. (*The Hollow Needle*)

November. Juve helps Fantômas escape from his Belgian prison. (*Fantômas 12: Le Magistrat Cambrioleur*)

November-December. Beautrelet, Ganimard and Holmes are not so easily thwarted. Separately, both Beautrelet and Holmes solve the mystery of the Needle. During the final battle, Raymonde is killed when she throws herself in front of Lupin to save him from a bullet fired by Holmes. Lupin, wracked with grief, manages to escape. (*The Hollow Needle*).

December. Fantômas robs an American millionaire (*Fantômas 13: La Livrée du Crime*)

1910.

January. Fantômas returns to New York to plan the theft of the SS *Triumph*. While there, he tangles with Nick Carter. (*Nick Carter vs. Fantômas*)

February. Juve and Fandor thwart the *Triumph* robbery. (*Fantômas 14: La Mort de Juve*)

March. Fantômas impersonates Juve. (*Fantômas 15: L'Evadée de Saint-Lazare*)

April. Juve and Fandor dismantle Fantômas' smuggling ring on the Spanish border. (*Fantômas 16: La Disparition de Fandor*)

Harry Dickson spends some time in New York visiting his cousin, Frederick Dickson. (*Fantômas in America*)

May. Back in England, Fantômas decides to use Sho-Po to murder William Beltham. Fantômas arranges to meet Sho-Po at the Johnsons' house.

June. Fantômas releases Bom-Ko, who kills a woman in Lyndhurst. The *Matilda Briggs* arrives in Southampton with Sho-Po still disguised as Bill Sharper.

The Man in Grey begins.